FLIGHT INTO FOLLY

FLIGHT INTO FOLLY

JON CHRISTENSEN

authorHOUSE®

AuthorHouse™
1663 Liberty Drive
Bloomington, IN 47403
www.authorhouse.com
Phone: 1-800-839-8640

Published by AuthorHouse   06/26/2012

ISBN: 978-1-4772-3201-9 (sc) ·
ISBN: 978-1-4772-3202-6 (e)

Library of Congress Control Number: 2012911453

DEDICATION

I would like to dedicate this book to all the countless people of either gender and any age who have been killed, physically wounded, emotionally maimed, or otherwise adversely affected by war, which is the ultimate act of man's inhumanity to man.

ACKNOWLEDGEMENTS

To my wife, Lyn, for her unflagging patience with the tedious process of proofreading, positive criticism, and ongoing encouragement.

To Stephen King for the invaluable help he afforded writers like me with his book, *On Writing—A Memoir of the Craft.*

(Oh see what you have wrought, Stephen.)

To all those countless authors who have laboured so diligently on the subject of the Vietnamese "conflict," just so that I might be provided with invaluable grist for my own particular mill.

To all the many editors from whom I received rejection letters, because they only succeeded in spurring me on to greater effort with their apparent obtuseness.

With special thanks to USAF Airman First Class (retired) Bob Sherman for making the aircraft photos available.

Last, but far from least: to you, Dear Readers, for exhibiting your exemplary taste in good literature by purchasing and/or reading this offering of mine.

AUTHOR'S FOREWORD

Since wisdom and learning are virtually synonymous and are largely dependent on experiences, I think that it could go without saying that no one can endure an experience without becoming at least a little wiser.

This is a story of just such an event. It was an event of enduring an experience. It was an event that generated some wisdom, though the realisation of that wisdom, at least by the protagonist, was somewhat belated. I think it is so very unfortunate that the acquisition of wisdom is too seldom the conscious goal of undertaking any course of action.

It is a story concerning a war, but the war is merely the vehicle by which the protagonist's wisdom is finally and consciously realised.

It's a rough riding vehicle to be sure (not wholly unlike the PTV mentioned in this story), but a vehicle nonetheless that so many thousands of men and women have ridden to the unwitting realisation of a greater wisdom. However that wisdom expands or enriches a person's life is, quite naturally, dependent on what that individual chooses to make of it.

This story, though written in the first person, is fiction and not autobiographical, as it might seem. Because it is fiction, a great deal of research was necessary for its creation. As with any work of fiction, although a fair amount of literary license has been taken in its development, the results of the research are what will, hopefully, make the story believable and therefore more acceptable—if not more enjoyable and, conceivably, thought provoking.

Most of the feelings and beliefs of that *first person* character were also my own during the period leading up to his enlistment. Moreover, some of those feelings and beliefs I still hold to this day. I think it may go without saying, then, that I've drawn heavily on my own experiences in life to outline the personality, if not the unwitting and rather foolhardy courage that this character chooses to exhibit.

We surely cannot live side by side with a people so closely related to us in history, commerce, trade, and traditions, without realising that certain feelings, expectations, dreams and conflicts of the one must surely impact the other for good or bad. Therefore, I believe it cannot be successfully argued that it wouldn't be in everyone's best interest to try and make that impact as positive as possible for as close to the majority as possible.

That realisation and understanding will hopefully show through in the decisions and actions of the story's main character, not to mention one or two of the other characters.

In writing this story about a very small part of the Vietnam conflict, it was obviously not my intention to write a definitive history of the event. That has already been done many times, as I was thankful to discover while conducting my research. In part, my aim was to draw attention to what seems to me to be a rather apparent parallel between it and what, at the time of writing, is occurring in the Middle East with American involvement (and some might say major instigation), and how the chances of success there are likely no greater than they were in Vietnam, and for many of the same reasons.

Another intention of mine was to bring to light the fact that there were many, largely shouted down and otherwise verbally or physically harassed and abused, ironically at *peace* rallies, who had a very democratic right to feel quite differently than those who, in my opinion, viewed the entire question with linear and narrow-minded thinking. Many of those who dared to voice unpopular views were the ones who, rightly or wrongly, for altruistic motives or not, had the strength of conviction to put their very lives on the line for their country and for their ideals, as opposed to those who merely stood on the sidelines spouting a blend of platitudes and verbal vitriol and so blindly denigrating, without any positive input, the actions and beliefs of those others. That, and to attempt to put faces (albeit fictitious faces) to some of the participants in that particular practice in madness as well as bringing again to focus the largely untold suffering that such a conflict inevitably and invariably inflicts on participants and civilians alike.

It always amazes me that we have evolved so far, immodestly celebrating our very limited part in the process, and still don't seem to have developed the ability to resolve disputes in a more humane, reasonable, and responsible manner where at all possible.

The old adage of *know thine enemy* is as valid now as when it was first coined so long ago. As a matter of fact, the first law of combat (if it must come to that) is: *know thine enemy*. The Americans, especially, seemed to have forgotten that. The Americans and their allies do not, and did not, know their enemies, not really, and certainly not in a sense that could have made and will make all the difference to the outcome. Therefore, regardless of their prodigious military might, I feel that the Americans and their allies are probably doomed to failure in what appears to be their latest folly.

A frontal assault war cannot successfully be waged against the guerrilla tactics of an enemy. It would be not unlike trying to push air into a box. The validity of that assertion is borne out by the history of military combat. In cases where guerrilla tactics invariably confounded and overwhelmed confrontations with even well trained and highly disciplined armies of some significant numbers, that validity is brought home even more forcefully.

The Romans learned that. Hell, the ancient Greeks learned it; not to mention the likes of Napoleon Bonaparte and Adolf Hitler, who also and perhaps fortunately learned the lesson far too late, if at all.

Even as the first rule of combat was initially disregarded, any wisdom that should have been gained from involvement in that first debacle in Vietnam certainly does not seem to have been employed before commencing with the involvement in the second in Afghanistan.

Of all the plethora of books that analyze wars, and particularly the Vietnam conflict and, more recently, the Iraq and Afghanistan wars, in my opinion the one that did it the best was probably Kenneth J. Campbell's *A Tale of Two Quagmires—Iraq, Vietnam and the hard lessons of war.* For me that was particularly true because of the close comparisons he made between the fiasco in Vietnam and what, at the time of writing this, is going on in the Middle East. In his book, he very aptly refers to those events as the "two quagmires."

The American people, especially, have been bogged down in two very costly quagmires, one of which certainly didn't end well and the other of which there's every indication that it won't end particularly well, either. Of course as always the main cost in such events is tallied in human misery and human life.

Perhaps, just perhaps, if the adage of *know thine enemy* was taken to heart by would be combatants, there wouldn't be any need for combat at all.

Jon Christensen

The god of war is drunk with blood,
The earth doth faint and fail;
The stench of blood makes sick the heavens;
Ghosts glut the throat of hell!

—Gwin, King of Norway

*   *   *

My argument is that War makes a rattling good
history; but Peace is poor reading.

—Thomas Hardy

*   *   *

"Now tell us all about the war,
And what they fought each other for."

—Robert Southey

*   *   *

After each war there is a little less democracy to save.

—Brooks Atkinson

* * *

When war is declared, Truth is the first casualty.

—attributed to US Senator Hiram Warren
Johnson—1918

* * *

Make love not war.

—Student and peace activist slogan—1960's

* * *

CHAPTER 1

It was a drawn out and full blown yell that brought me up out of the engulfing darkness of unconsciousness; a protracted yell that seemed to have been generated by a gripping and near crippling terror. It seemed to have come from some far off source, and yet somehow I knew, in my cloudy, resurfacing consciousness, that it had been generated within me.

My head felt as though it was floating apart from my body. At the same time, it felt packed-to-bursting with sodden cotton wool. I had a vague impression my tongue had been glued to the roof of my mouth, and try as I may, I couldn't seem to dislodge it. However, my sense of taste didn't appear to have been impaired, and what I was tasting then was anything but pleasant. It was as though I had been dining on carrion for some considerable length of time without the benefit of mouthwash. The odour of my breath must have been like that of a hyena after a glutinous feast on something in an extremely advanced stage of decomposition.

Something in an advanced stage of decomposition seemed to niggle at the outer reaches of my memory, but I wasn't yet quite conscious enough to grasp what it might be. Whatever it was, I had presence of mind enough to realise it would probably be anything but pleasant.

I was awake, or at least aware, but everything was shifting shapes of varying shades of grey. Then there was a slight pressure on my left eyelid, a sudden flicker of glaring white light, and a female voice saying something that my foggy mind couldn't quite understand. I instinctively turned my throbbing head away from the annoying light source and the pressure on my eyelid.

"Well, doctor, it looks like he's finally coming around," said the female voice as a sudden sense of coherency flooded to my brain.

The almost seductive sound of her rather silkily husky and well modulated voice had a strangely comforting effect on me, and I hoped she would say more regardless of whether or not I might understand it. I wanted, almost desperately, to see the owner of that voice.

With a great effort, I forced my sticky eyelids to part. I had only just accomplished that when a male voice stole my attention: "So, you've decided to join us again. Good. You've slept quite enough for one week, mister. Do you know where you are?" the voice asked in somewhat less melodic tones than those of his associate.

With no small amount of exertion, I blinked my gritty eyelids a few times to try and clear my vision and then, turning my head towards the sound of that voice, my eyes slowly focused on a craggy, lined, and well-tanned face topped with a tousle of curly white hair and sporting a cock-eyed smile hampered somewhat by a nasty looking scar running from the corner of his mouth to the base of his ear lobe. With a concerted effort, I focused on the stethoscope dangling from his neck and on the white lab coat that he wore.

"A hospital would be my first guess," I said in a forced croak that I hardly recognised as my own voice.

I also noted that the doctor was a major in the Medical Corps, and I was so impressed that I would have saluted had I been able to lift my arm. As it was, all I could manage was a weak grin of appreciation. His smile straightened and broadened slightly and the scar brightened slightly as well.

Then I recalled to my still fuzzy consciousness that seductive female voice and visually sought out the source on the other side of the bed. You know how the mental image that you generate for yourself from the sound of a voice is rarely the same as what it actually is? Well, that was certainly the case in this instance; though not unpleasantly so.

The source of that enchanting voice was a fairly tall, Rubenesque blonde in a crisp blue dress with a starched white pinafore apron. She looked strong enough to have packed me around like a baby. Gone like a mist in a gale was the mental image of a sloe-eyed, lissom and full, pouty lipped Arabian nights belly dancer with waist length ebony hair. There certainly didn't seem to be much wrong with my imagination.

As she looked down at me with sparkling eyes that matched the colour of her dress and crinkled at the outer corners with laugh lines, she grinned from ear to ear as though she had just become a proud, new parent. Who knows, maybe the broad grin was because she had read my mind. I kind of hoped not.

"I think he's going to make it, Doctor," she said in that golden, honeyed voice, and her chubby, pink cheeks dimpled prettily with her smile.

"We'll have a longer chat later, Corporal," he said in a tone suddenly as crisp as the nurse's apron. Maybe he had read my mind as well. "We can start him on solid food this afternoon, nurse."

"Yes, Doctor," she said. Then to me: "Luncheon will be served at 1300 hours, *m'lord*."

With that she drew back the bed curtains, fluffed up my pillows, and gave me a sip of water through a bent glass straw in a blue plastic tumbler, while the doctor hastily wrote a few notes on a chart and hung it on the foot of my bed. As the nurse bustled around me, her fresh, clean scent wafted over me till I thought I was falling in love. It had seemed a very long time indeed since I'd smelled anything that clean and fresh. Then they briskly walked out of the room, leaving me in a sudden void to examine my new surroundings, at least visually.

I was to see my Rubenesque angel of mercy only once more during my stay. That was when she reappeared later that day to remove the Foley catheter that had been monitoring my hydration and kidney function. It was hardly the form of intimacy that I had been fantasising about, however the fantasies continued unabated for some time anyway. That was probably a good indicator of my returning health and vitality.

On that occasion, she also brought me a small tube of mint-flavoured toothpaste, a toothbrush, and a small bottle of mouthwash, which was probably a good indicator of the state of my breath and, embarrassingly, that she was very likely aware of it.

From the looks of it, I had spent the week in a long room painted in two shades of restful, pale green with a narrow dark green stripe separating the upper from the lower colours. I noted seven other beds in the room, only two others which were currently occupied. There was evidence to indicate, however, that the five others were only temporarily unoccupied.

From a pale blue sky, the sun was shining through four tall, narrow windows at the far end of the room, and three fans, down the centre of the white tiled ceiling, were lazily stirring the air. In time, I could have told you how many tiles there were in that ceiling and how many holes in each tile—not to mention the stain in one corner that resembled nothing less than Abraham Lincoln's profile.

A man in one of the end beds by the windows was bandaged from his head and as far down as I could see. One plaster encased leg was elevated and held in place by what appeared to be plastic-coated cables attached to an overhead bar and pulley contraption. There was no obvious evidence of the existence of a second leg beneath the sheet. From a tubular metal stand on one side of his bed hung two IV bags from which tubes led downwards, their destination being shrouded from full view by his bed sheet. On the other side of his bed was a rather ominous-looking tall, black box whose miniature green and amber lights flickered in time to the soft, rhythmic beeps emanating from it. From this box several thin, black cables extended down and also disappeared beneath the sheet.

Poor bugger! I thought. He looked a lot worse off than I felt.

I then looked down at my own body. My hands and gauze-swathed arms were all still there, with fingers intact, though there was a clear, flexible plastic tube running from a liquid filled bag over my head and into my left arm via a taped down needle. I looked towards the foot of my bed, flexed my sheet shrouded feet and wiggled my toes—all apparently present and accounted for, and obviously still in working order. Then as I twisted slightly, I suddenly became sharply aware that my left side hurt like hell, and in a sudden, mild panic, I wondered what that was all about. No one had told me exactly what was the matter with me.

That sharp pain must have prodded my memory, because very slowly, some impressions started coming back to me. I remembered being in a Medevac Huey chopper. The rhythm of the rotating blades overhead had beat time to the thrumming in my throbbing, feverish head. There had been shouting voices all around in an atmosphere of stifling heat and fleeting visions of different, perspiration dripping faces peering down at me. For some reason, I remembered a drip of sweat dropping from the tip of someone's nose and hitting me right between the eyes. Then there was a sweet, all engulfing blackness.

I had woken up in a plane, I think. Then, after awaking from yet another spell of unconsciousness, there was a confused impression of crowded bustling and fresh, salty-sweet air, brilliant sunlight, and a slight breeze that had felt so incredibly refreshing. Then there had been that welcoming black void again. And now, here; but where was *here*?

My confused musings were interrupted as I suddenly became acutely aware that I was being rather intently scrutinised by the propped-up occupant of a bed directly across from me. When he noticed me glance in his direction, his face seemed to brighten considerably from its previous knit browed expression of acute and seemingly concerned concentration.

"Well, howdy there, fella!" It was a gravelly yet slightly high-pitched male voice from that bed directly across from mine. The man's pock-marked face had the thin features of a hawk with a matching hawk-billed nose and piercing, dark eyes. His sharp, prominent Adam's apple bobbled vigorously as he spoke, and I found that strangely amusing.

"You bin makin' quite the ruckus there, fella. How ya doin'?"

"Oh, uh, *howdy*," I said, trying to emulate his style of address because of my embarrassment. "I hope I haven't been keeping you off your sleep."

"Naw, naw, ya git used t'it in this place."

It sounded like he'd said used *tit*, and I smiled in spite of myself. He grinned broadly back, showing large, yellowed teeth and obviously misunderstanding the reason for my smile.

"But ya musta had a time of it, though. Where 'bouts you come in from?" he continued.

"'Nam," I said automatically, "Saigon . . . yah, Saigon." Then it was all flooding back to me. "Yah, I've just come in from Tan Son Nhut. But where are we now?"

"Why, we's in paradise, fella." Then, seeing the quizzical look on my face, he said, "Naw, naw, we ain't daid, we's on Oahu—thet's in Hawaii, ya know. I never bin before, and damned if it din't take a war to git me here. I kin hardly wait t'git my toes in thet warm, white san' and take a dip in the surf with some sweet li'l *wahine*," he waxed dreamily.

Good luck to you, I thought, trying in vain to picture that rather fierce-looking, pock-marked, southern hillbilly with "some sweet li'l *wahine*". Good luck, indeed! *Poor girl* was an afterthought.

So, we were in Hawaii. I was halfway home. At that realisation, tears welled up unbidden in my eyes, and thankfully, my talkative new pal from across the way fell silent. He was probably contemplating the surf, sand, and sweet little wahine, as he resumed his rather rapt perusal of a very dog-eared *Hustler* magazine, the pages of which he flipped with one hand while the other one was suspiciously occupied beneath his sheet. I felt a sudden pang of pity for whoever it was that would have to change his bed linen.

Shaking that thought off, my attention turned instead to thoughts of home: Mom's home cooked meals on Sundays, hanging out on weekends with my old pals, the smell of *cool* rain on the trees of Stanley Park, or just vegging out on the beach at Spanish Banks or English Bay with a good book and the view of well oiled and bronzed, bikini clad women against golden sand and emerald water. I suddenly realised how much I'd missed all of that as well as the view of eternally snow-capped mountains—and most of my former life that I had been so determined to leave behind.

I would have to write home as soon as I could manage it. It had been almost three months (it seemed an eternity longer) since I had sent my last letter.

Letters from the "theatre of operations" were always scrupulously censored, but even at that you had to be rather circumspect about what you wrote. As a result, you couldn't really impart anything but the banal and inconsequential. Who knows what the military may have told my family about my current situation. My mom, at least, deserved to know where and how I was; or at the very least that I was still alive and to have some tangible proof of it.

CHAPTER 2

Until 1960, the United States had merely supported the Saigon regime in South Vietnam with about seven hundred advisors for the purpose of training the South Vietnamese army. Out of what was felt a necessity, that number had grown steadily. Until by late 1964, the numbers had swelled to some twenty-three thousand American combat troops.

As no military headway was being made by the South Vietnamese Army and, ostensibly because the North Vietnamese had attacked US ships in 1964, President Lyndon Johnson had ordered bombing raids on North Vietnamese targets in early 1965. Then, in March of 1965, he also sent in thirty-five hundred U.S. Marine combat troops. Those troops were initially sent to defend the air base at Danang. However, later in 1965, two-hundred thousand U.S. troops were committed to begin an offensive set of battles and break the back of Viet Cong resistance.

From about August of 1965, Viet Cong guerrilla tactics began in earnest. This marked the beginning of the end of any U.S. successes in the field, and the beginning of a U.S. troop frustration that only escalated until it eventually led to some of the worst atrocities of the entire conflict. A lot of what went on in Vietnam in those days not only flew in the face of the Geneva Convention on Civilian Protection, but also the United Nation ratified Rules of Land Warfare.

Although the U.S. never officially declared war on North Vietnam, it passed the Gulf of Tonkin Resolution, which was, in effect, a *back door* sort of declaration. This resolution gave authorisation to the U.S. forces in South East Asia to repel any further attacks and to prevent further aggression in whatever manner seemed most appropriate to accommodate an eventual victory.

Ostensibly, the gloves were off and anything went.

Thus U.S. bombings of so called North Vietnamese *strategic sites* not only continued, but actually escalated over the next couple of years. By 1968, the U.S. military complement had grown to half a million strong backed by some six hundred thousand South Vietnamese troops and almost a hundred thousand from other south Pacific countries.

The North Vietnamese Communist forces NVA), at that time, numbered about two hundred and thirty-five thousand troops. However, countless more guerrilla fighters were enlisted by the Viet Cong from the ranks of peasant farmers and itinerants, even in the south. There is no actual record of how many guerrilla fighters there were in all, however conservative though unofficial estimates peg the numbers in the tens of thousands.

After Richard Nixon became president in 1968, he began cutting back on U.S. troop deployment to the area due to increasing public pressure at home and the beginning of the on again off again peace negotiations in Paris. The public relations on the home front really began a very serious deterioration after the Tet offensive in January of 1968. In July of 1969, the U.S. Army began actual troop withdrawals. This continued until 1972, by which time there were fewer than seventy thousand directly involved in the conflict, which in turn resulted in a higher U.S. casualty rate. At least some of the casualty rate was due to an American invention euphemistically referred to as "friendly fire". This developed, in large part, because by that stage the troops were extremely stressed and very nervous, notwithstanding, or perhaps because of the burgeoning use of drugs amongst them.

In 1973, the Paris Peace Accords, which had finally been signed and ratified, required the withdrawal of all but fifty military personnel. Those fifty were to remain in an advisory capacity only. However, hostilities didn't come to an actual end until two years later when North Vietnam's complete victory was finally realised with the capture of Saigon.

Later that same year, when the cease fire wasn't being strictly observed and the withdrawal wasn't being carried out with the alacrity deemed fitting, Canada ostentatiously withdrew as a member of the international commission supervising the accords.

It was fairly obvious that no one had considered the magnitude, ramifications, and logistical difficulties involved in securing a disentanglement and withdrawal as rapid as the peace accord had dictated. It must be remembered that, right or wrong, just or not, that conflict had gone on for decades. There had been discord between the North and the South long before the Americans became involved.

Long before U.S. involvement, when it became apparent that the South Vietnamese were going to have to capitulate to the giant Communist military machine of the North (backed by Peking, now known as Beijing), the French stepped in to try and broker a settlement one way or another (and, admittedly, protect their own investments in the area and re-impose colonial rule). The virtually inevitable and resultant conflict practically decimated the French military, not to mention the devastating effect it had on the French economy, regardless of the U.S. financial aid for the enterprise.

The conflict between North and South Vietnam was preceded by the Indo-China War of 1946 to 1954 between France and the Viet Minh. After all those years of frustrating and costly conflict, they suffered a humiliating defeat at Dien Bien Phu and were forced to withdraw leaving a gap the Americans felt compelled to fill some time later and after they showed the South Koreans how to govern themselves.

Not only was Vietnam divided into North and South, but the South itself was divided into no fewer than four parts with anything but distinct boundaries. There was one area controlled by the National Front for the Liberation of Vietnam (NLF); another scattered group of areas controlled by the U.S. and Saigon government troops; a huge area, mostly in the North, controlled by Pathet Lao; and yet another disjointed group of areas that were in a constant state of dispute. It would have been of immense benefit to the South if it could have been united in some semblance of cohesion.

It should be explained that Pathet Lao was the Laotian nationalist movement whose principal function it was to fight for a republic status in their homeland. It wasn't until 1975 that Laos ceased to be a monarchy. However, the question has to be asked: what business did they have controlling parts of an already divided country that had not the slightest semblance of influence in whether or not they became a republic?

It also needs to be remembered that the Americans had been intensely embroiled in the "Cold War" for some not inconsiderable length of time. The U.S. was the main protagonist and Communist paranoia was rife in the States. They saw a virulent expansionist world Communist movement afoot. and if they could deny another global slice to the Communists, then they would feel vindicated in their eyes as well as those of the rest of the free world. At best, it was a very fine balancing act. At worst, it could all have ended in World War III and global devastation. In short, it was a situation not without considerable stress for governments and general population alike.

However, the U.S. military position in the world wouldn't allow them any other option but involvement; and an involvement, it must be realised, that had the tacit and hopeful approval of most of the free world, at least at the outset. It must be acknowledged that had the Americans won in Vietnam, the common attitude towards their involvement there would have been vastly different. After all, everyone loves a winner . . .

As it was, by the latter days of the conflict, a movement of anti-Vietnam war veterans called the Vietnam Veterans Against the War (VVAW) had been formed and become quite active. Their conscience driven goal was to bring a badly faltering conflict to an end by any means, short of anarchy, that they could. With public sympathies favouring their message, they were generally quite successful in their endeavours.

Finally, after years of bitter and bloody battles, the North Vietnamese victoriously entered Saigon at the end of April 1975 and a flurry of final, frantic evacuations ensued. It was, not to put too fine a point on it, pandemonium, bedlam, and utter chaos. The battles, it seemed, were not yet at a complete end as thousands more were killed, maimed, or injured in the last mad rush and stampede to freedom in whatever direction it could possibly be found.

In 1976, North and South Vietnam were united under a Communist government, as *The Socialist Republic of Vietnam*, and Saigon, in the south, was renamed *Ho*

Chi Minh City after a Communist North Vietnamese political icon.

By the end of the conflict, almost three million Americans had served between August of 1964 and May of 1975. Some sixty thousand were killed, three hundred thousand wounded, and seventy-five thousand were permanently disabled. Another twenty-five thousand were listed as missing in action. An inordinately large number of the missing were never found or heard from again.

In all, the U.S. involvement included all four military corps, organised into twelve divisions; two thousand aircraft, and fifteen hundred naval vessels. While all of that may sound very impressive, in actual fact there was only about fifteen percent of all U.S. troops in Vietnam that were ever actually involved in sustained combat throughout the entire conflict. All the rest of the military complement were involved in support functions such as driving, supply administration, intelligence gathering, troop coordination, and the like. In short, the typical inverted triangle power structure.

For Canadian and other foreign enlistees, a three-year enlistment and a twelve-month tour of duty in South East Asia were required. The Canadian Foreign Enlistment Act, which was meant to deny Canadian citizens the right to enlist for foreign military service, was ignored by the Canadian government because, initially, there was an obvious if tacit approval of U.S. involvement in South Vietnam. One may well wonder why then, after Canada withdrew from the International Commission for Peace, it still turned a blind eye to a foreign enlistment policy that it had felt strongly enough about to pass into law. Even after Canada's almost self-righteous posturing on the world stage because of the pressure of popular opinion, it still seemed tacitly to have approved of the U.S. involvement.

CHAPTER 3

At the outset, I'd like it understood that I am a Canadian citizen. I was born and bred as such and am unabashedly proud of the fact. Having said that, there have been times, even to the present, when I have felt my pride has been sorely tested by the actions of some few Canadians—most of those present in positions of parliamentary power. I do recognise and question the shortcomings, but regardless of all of that, my pride remains intact still.

I was twenty-seven years old in 1971, and ever since about 1967, when I first became aware of the exodus of draft dodgers flocking to Canada from the States, I had felt that something wasn't quite right with their apparent lack of patriotism. How could they not care about their own country's struggle? How could they apparently be so self centred and self serving?

In my late twenties, I still maintained some of that idealism usually peculiar only to teenagers, college students, and latter day hippies. For that reason, I felt that these draft dodgers were self-serving and cowardly in the face of their country's need. This belief certainly ran contrary to the idealism, mostly of teenagers, college students, and latter day hippies, on the other side of the argument.

In the news media and on the streets I had witnessed, with something approaching disgust, the anti-war demonstrations and riots by wild-eyed, wild-haired, frothing and flower fondling *peaceniks*, both in the States and increasingly in Canada.

I felt that no other country had the right to interfere in the internal affairs of the States, particularly in encouraging and accepting draft dodgers, which I saw as illegal immigration. The Canadian immigration authorities surreptitiously turned a blind eye to it all unless approached by the FBI. Only then did they bend to the will of extradition laws and assist with the arrest and deportation of the apparently well meaning miscreants.

It may seem that I was torn by an apparent conflict of beliefs, but I simply felt that if something was wrong then it was wrong no matter which faction perpetrated the deed. I just felt, and indeed recognised, that there were certainly wrongs perpetrated on both sides of the issue.

My beliefs were largely based on the fact that at least the Americans had been invited into South Vietnam to assist in their struggle against Communism, albeit the assistance was originally meant to be in the form of military advice and military training. At that point, the Vietnamese, at least, hadn't taken to shouting "Yankee, go home!" in the streets. That, however, was yet to come and based mainly on the frustrating failure of a speedy and successful conclusion to the conflict.

For the better part of two years, as I say, I had witnessed all of this with growing concern and mounting disgust. According to what the news media could accurately report of the matter, the States were not doing well in South East Asia, and I attributed that, in large part, to what I viewed as the cowardly and self-serving acts of draft dodgers and deserters; there were thousands of them. It was all feverishly being spurred on by high profile celebrities like Jane Fonda, Bob Dylan, Arlo Guthrie, and their ilk. All of their self-aggrandised public protests and misguided rhetoric, I was certain, was for the sole purpose of furthering their own selfish agendas.

As time wore on, an idea began to germinate in my idealistic mind. Canadians and some from other countries, notably Australia, had gone to the aid of the States by enlisting for the fight against what was deemed to be the expansionist world Communist movement. Why, then, shouldn't I do the same? Because *if you're not part of the solution, you're part of the problem*, as a common saying went. Idealism, I felt, was futile and impotent if not backed up by action.

For the better part of a year, I had pondered the idea of enlisting. However, perhaps understandably, there were some niggling questions in my mind. How would I handle the almost dead certainty of being shipped to Vietnam? By that time, I had become aware that the Paris Peace Accords, though not yet complete and ratified, had demanded the withdrawal of troops from the area, and yet military personnel were still being shipped over. Hostile conflict was still going on. What

were the chances of my survival? How would I cope
with the idea of having to kill someone if I was sent
over? What sort of reception would my action elicit
on the home front? To what attitude would I return
and what form would that attitude take? I had seen
returning military personnel being harassed, assaulted,
and actually spat on in the streets.

All these questions and more spun dizzyingly around my
mind and sorely challenged my idealism. My reasons
for wanting to go, however, were still immutable.

Then I realised these were probably some of the very
same questions asked by those who chose to desert or
simply dodge the draft. Should I lump myself in with
those types? How, having done so, could I live with
myself when there was something I could have done?

Although I would be going in at what would prove to
be the tail end of events over there, I felt at the time
there was still something I could and should be doing,
no matter the delay.

Although there was something called the Canadian
Foreign Enlistment Act in Canada that was ostensibly
supposed to stop Canadian citizens from joining
any foreign military, it didn't seem to be deterring
Canadians from enlisting in the U.S. military. As a
matter of fact, the Canadian government seemed to
be turning a blind eye to it right across the country.
To me, this appeared tantamount to tacit approval, and
therefore nothing stood in my way except to think it
through and decide—easy enough to say.

By that time, I had found out that I didn't need to become an American citizen to enlist; not unless I ever wanted to acquire a commission as an officer. That didn't appeal to me enough to give up my Canadian citizenship. For general enlistment, I would merely be issued with what amounted to a landed immigrant card, present myself at a U.S. recruitment centre, and that was basically it.

I felt that my life to that point had been incredibly dull and uneventful. I was practically bordering on thirty with nothing of consequence having been accomplished in my life. Surely there was more to life than plodding away in some dead end job and looking forward only to a weekend of partying and social posturing at a night club like *Oil Can Harry's,* or *Dirty Sal's Cellar*, or the odd house party. All this for the dubious delights afforded by booze, some questionable pleasures derived by engaging in gratuitous sex, and other sundry high jinks.

There were no serious love interests for me, either current or on the horizon. What did I really have to lose? Perhaps surprisingly, the event of my own possible death or dismemberment hadn't, at that point, made the transition from subconscious to conscious thought. Anyway, I had always tended to roll with what I deemed the punches of life. My attitude had always been: *If something's going to happen, it will happen.* Kismet, I guess you'd call it.

CHAPTER 4

"What in hell do you mean by thinking you should join up in the Yank army?"

"It was just a thought, Dad," I said more by way of waylaying a pointless argument, than allaying any actual fearful concern he might have had. From a lifetime of experience, I knew only too well what his attitude would most likely be, and here came the proof of the pudding yet again.

"Well, not a very clear thought, I think. The Yanks got themselves into that bloody mess; let them get themselves out of it. Anyway, what in Hell's horn do you think *you* could do?"

That last bit, with the emphasis on *you*, stung my already withered ego. However, although I deliberately decided to take it as a rhetorical question, I wouldn't have deigned to answer it in any case. Any possible answer I may have given would've succeeded only in prolonging a pointless discussion that, admittedly, I had initiated by daring to think out loud in the first place. I should've learned by that time that I couldn't think out loud around Dad—not if I didn't want to be put in the unenviable position of vainly having to defend my point of view to him.

For some long while, I had thought that I had been something of a disappointment to Dad. Our work ethics, for one example, were definitely at odds. While he lived for his job, I considered mine as merely a means to an end. In the beginning, that was enough. Then, as nothing monetarily more appealing or cerebrally more challenging appeared on the horizon, it was not nearly enough for me. It just seemed that my life was trickling away from me.

In any case, there were only three ways of doing anything in that household: the right way, the wrong way and Dad's way. In my dad's view, there was only his way. In that regard alone, I felt justified in believing that dear old Dad was one of the punches of life with which I had learned to roll.

With the notion of avoiding any further acrimony (at least for the time being), I thanked them for the supper, kissed Mom goodnight, and left—discretion always being the better part of valour.

"Think about what in hell you're doing, boy!" was Dad's parting shot, accompanied by one of his best searing glares.

"Please, son," was Mom's, accompanied by a wan, pleading smile.

I merely gave a non-committal wave as I continued on my way.

Mom probably felt that I was too *sensitive* for such an undertaking. I knew she'd always tried her best, though not always successfully, to shelter me from Dad's overbearing ways while I was growing up. Perhaps she thought she'd done too good a job of it.

Dad had a very old European idea of his role as head of *his* household. In that regard, the definition of democracy was denied a presence in his lexicon. Consideration of ideas other than his own wasn't consciously entertained. There was to be no captain-cum-helmsman of his ship but him. I always suspected that the infamous Captain Bligh, of *Mutiny on the Bounty* renown, would have been a hero in his eyes. I can clearly recall him passing comments of ardent admiration for the overbearing and ill-fated captain after we had watched the film on television.

He didn't seem to understand that I was no longer aboard *his* ship; that I was no longer a "boy"; and that he wasn't Captain Bligh and I wasn't Fletcher Christian. I was attempting to construct and captain a ship of my own, and it seemed to me he resented the loss of control. Now he only had Mom at home to control, although she seemed to be bearing the bitter brunt of it quite stoically.

Perhaps ironically, his own father had had many of the same iron handed attitudes, for which he hated him enough to leave the old country on the cusp of the Great Depression and at the tender age of eighteen. The decision between Canada and Argentina had been decided by the toss of a coin, he had smugly confessed.

So much for captaining your own ship and grasping fate by the throat!

I didn't hate my father; I just felt a little sorry for him and for the accumulation of things he'd likely missed out on because of all the unbending convictions that he held as sacrosanct.

I used to think about that coin toss. If the coin had come up the other way and he had gone to Argentina, would I have been Mom's son or his? Or would neither of them have had kids? Well, that would certainly have solved what, at times like this, I viewed as my problems.

Perhaps Dad and I were just too much alike in some ways. He had tried to enlist in 1941. His convictions and I feel unwarranted gratitude to his adopted country, dictated that he should defend the principles for which that adopted country stood. He would have made it, too, had it not been for the hernia the induction board medics had discovered. In that regard, the only difference between him and me was that I didn't have a wife to leave behind.

"*Think about what in hell you're doing, boy.*" Indeed! I'd thought about it long and hard. My decision wouldn't be made by the bloody toss of a coin, and *that* was another difference between the two of us.

What could *I* do? Maybe, just maybe I'd show them all, or show *him* at the very least. It didn't occur to me until years later that *showing him* must have been at least one of the subconscious reasons for making the decision that I eventually made.

By the second circuit around the block on foot, I had cooled down enough to climb into my car and drive off. *To hell with it all,* I thought. *There's still time to catch up with the gang at the pub.* And I did, only to my painful regret the following morning as I stumbled in to make it for seven a.m. strike picket duty at the plant. For the rest of that day, I could dwell only on the unrelenting and crushing hangover, the rancid taste in my mouth, and the acrid churning of my stomach.

Never again, I vowed yet again.

My decision was irrevocably made the following day, when I could once again think coherently without invoking pounding cranial pains. I even started a journal to document my coming adventure, and hopefully the entire story. Perhaps my last confrontation with Dad had been the deciding factor in finally making up my mind in such a seemingly precipitous manner. To this day, I'm not at all sure.

CHAPTER 5

Tuesday, September 7, 1971

Well, Diary, I've done it! Yesterday morning I drove myself down to Seattle and joined the U.S. Army Corp. It was surprisingly matter-of-fact and painless. I might have been a patriotic American citizen, as far as they were concerned. They gave me a physical on the spot, asked me a few questions (mostly about political affiliations), made me swear allegiance to the President, the flag, etc., etc. for the duration of my enlistment, and told me that I'd be notified to report for duty within ten days. That was it! I was in and out of there in about two hours. At the risk of self denigration, I couldn't help thinking they must have been desperate. I celebrated by stopping off at *The Canadian* in Blaine, on the way back, for a beer, burger, and a half pound tin of Middleton's Cherry Blend pipe tobacco.

Friday, September 10, 1971

The usual post-strike mad scramble at work today. We finally got the last bit of crap cleared up after the strike. Four shifts are now in full swing, and we're churning out product like crazy and playing catch-up with a backlog of orders. I'm just pleased that I'm a fork-lift operator in shipping and nowhere near the production line—shipping is crazy enough! As usual, I'm looking forward to the weekend.

Monday, September 13, 1971

Twenty-seven forty footers and B-trains loaded today. A record! Also a personal record of just under two minutes to load a forty footer. I had my military notification waiting for me when I got home. A very official looking letter in a plain, buff envelope from the U.S. State Department thanked me, rather gushingly I thought, for my laudable patriotism in the struggle against Communism. They also informed me that I was expected to report for duty at 0800 hours (I'll have to get used to the twenty-four hour clock) at Fort Bragg, north of San Francisco, on Monday, October 4, 1971. Transport would be provided from Seattle Air Force Base at 1600 hours the day before. I briefly thought it was a bit odd that I wasn't being sent to Fort Lewis in Washington which was a lot closer to Vancouver. Anyway, it'll still give me time to arrange for a military leave-of-absence from work. Not that I really want to go back there, but since the union contract allows for it, I might as well take full advantage of it and hedge my bets, so to speak.

Tuesday, September 14, 1971

Today I spoke with the plant manager. To put it mildly, he wasn't overly enthused about having to hold my job for what might be three years. However, in the end, he had no option but to grant an official leave-of-absence for the duration of my military service. (The union contract doesn't make any mention of a particular country the military service was for—a loop-hole that I took full advantage of.) I was very careful not to stipulate a definite time frame except to agree that it would be for one term of service only. This company can be very devious about getting around such things. Now, I just have about two weeks to get the rest of my affairs in order; including a will, just in case . . .

Saturday, October 2, 1971

Well, Diary, the time has just flown by. This morning I packed a bag with immediate essentials and took a bus to Seattle. I found out where the Air Force base was and then just spent the rest of the time looking around the city. I went up the Space Needle and had lunch, browsed through the second-hand and pawn shops along First Avenue, and just generally whiled away the time. I had splashed out on a room at the Tropics, which was supposed to be one of the better hotels, then came across a pair of mating cockroaches in the bathroom vanity. The manager assured me that cockroaches could be found in some of the best hotels. I was highly sceptical, but let it slide. What the hell, they were rather entertaining after all.

Sunday, October 3, 1971

I made it to the Air Force base with about forty-five minutes to spare, which was just as well. There was a raft of checking and double checking to make sure I was a bona fide enlistee and not someone with devious motives. I guess they must have found it unusual that a Canadian would enlist, with the distinct possibility of being shipped to Vietnam. Anyway, I was finally cleared with about two minutes to flight time—and the military are a good deal more punctual with take-offs than are commercial air lines. The hatch was no sooner latched, and we began taxiing down the runway. There were twenty-three of us on board, and I was the only Canadian on the flight. We landed about two hours later, were processed, fed quite decently and then conducted to the barracks. Lights out at 2200 hours.

Monday, October 4, 1971

Well, Diary, here I am at Fort Bragg. They began processing us almost the minute we had stepped off the aircraft last night and it continued this morning at 0630 hours. We were issued fatigues (something like khaki pyjamas), nylon combat boots, socks, cap, even underwear (all khaki and two of everything), a backpack, and duffel bag (also khaki). Then came the haircut. Now I have more hair on my eyebrows and eyelids than on the top of my head. I guess styling doesn't loom large in their training. Then we assembled on the parade grounds for inspection and were introduced to our drill sergeant (Cummings or Collins, or something like that), who proclaimed us to be the saddest looking ragtag of misfits he had ever had the misfortune of being downwind of, etc.

Tuesday, October 5, 1971

Today we were taught to walk—or, more correctly, to march—with a backpack laden with fifty pounds of rocks. Someone on parade said that the rocks would certainly come in handy to throw at the enemy, for which infraction he was given a severe ten-minute tongue lashing and expected to do a hundred push-ups. Now, at least, we have a measure of Sergeant Cummings or Collins. Too wasted to write more just now.

Sunday, October 10, 1971

Well, Diary, here I am again, at long last. This first week has been pretty much a whirlwind. I found out two things: there is no such thing as weekends off in the military, and we are all expected to attend religious services in the denomination of our choice, well, Christian or Jewish, as it turns out. This, regardless of avowed agnostic or atheist leanings. I will say that Sunday seems to be a little slacker, activity-wise, than the rest of the week. Oh yes, I found out something else, as well: Fort Bragg had been a military training facility in World War II, and then mothballed until the Korean war when it had been used as a munitions storage and distribution facility for a time. They dusted it off again as a training facility shortly after the beginning of the Vietnam "conflict," as they prefer to call it. Tomorrow we begin firearms training.

Monday, October 11, 1971

Well, this was a *fun* day! We spent the whole day learning how to disassemble and reassemble our firearms. Fortunately the M-16A1 is a surprisingly uncomplicated rifle, although some did have springs flying around the hangar much to the annoyance of

Sergeant Cumlings (yes, that's his name). Tomorrow we tackle the complexities of the .45 calibre semiautomatic sidearm. I wonder when we'll actually get to fire them.

Wednesday, October 13, 1971

Finally, today we were issued five twenty-round magazines ("clips," they call them) of .223 calibre live ammunition for the M-16. This rifle has been adapted with three settings: single fire, burst (three rounds at a trigger pull), and fully automatic (which, understandably, we were not allowed to use). It was only towards the end of the day that we were allowed to try the burst setting with our last "clip." Tomorrow we try our hands at the Colt .45 on the twenty yard range. Oh yeah! Like we'll be hitting any bull's eyes at twenty yards with a five inch barrelled handgun.

Friday, October 15, 1971

No more *soft* touches on the range. Today we donned our back packs (complete with fifty pounds of rocks), grabbed our rifles and "ran the course." This timed exercise comprised swinging hand-over-hand on an overhead lattice frame, swinging from rope to rope over a mud bog (shades of Tarzan), climbing over a series of twelve and sixteen foot plank walls, and crawling under a series of twenty foot long frames with barbed wire mesh about eighteen inches off the ground (fondly referred to, by Sergeant Cumlings, as the "ass graters"). To successfully accomplish this last feat, we first had to take off our back packs and push them and our rifles ahead of us. We didn't complete the course in the time thought appropriate, by the sergeant, for retarded chimpanzees. Tomorrow we go on a twenty mile hike in full "kit." It's always nice to have something to look forward to.

Sunday, October 17, 1971

Sorry, Diary, but I was just too wasted to write anything yesterday. Five of us dozed off in chapel this morning and got a hundred push-ups each for our temerity. At least we didn't have to do that with our packs of rocks . . . maybe the sergeant hasn't thought of that yet. Tomorrow, and for the rest of the week, it's more running the course and *strolls* in the *wilds.* I certainly hope that all these acquired *skills* prove to be useful in the future. I know now why they call the army corps "grunts." I'll write more when I catch my breath.

Sunday, October 24, 1971

Well, Diary, I never did catch my breath last week. At least I didn't fall asleep in chapel this morning. I hear that tomorrow, for those who may be interested (hey, we actually get a choice in something!), we can start parachute training. I'm not so sure if that's something that would *turn my crank*. Also, there will be a driver's course—now that sounds more like it!

Monday, October 25, 1971

Yes, Diary, they did have a driver's course. I signed up for that in a flash, otherwise I had heard that I might be "volunteered" for parachute training. Anyway, in the afternoon, I got out on the course in an old Willys Jeep with an NCO, Corporal Belkins, by my side. There were five Jeeps in a convoy and it was a bit like a day in the park, really. We drove on some rough, winding old logging roads and up and down some rather steep hills for a couple of hours and then returned to base. This is alright!

Tuesday, October 26, 1971

Christ, Diary, they were shooting at your boy today! Light arms and what seemed like mortar fire, for God's sake! Nobody ever told me that was part of the course. Of course, I did wonder why we were all issued with flak jackets and helmets this morning. Mind you, after the initial shock, it was kind of a blast. The corporal said I'd done quite well with the evasive driving. I told him it was a piece of cake, because, after all, I had driven in Montreal. Two of the others didn't fare so well, though, and a wrecker had to be sent out to retrieve a couple of wrecked Jeeps. The corporal said that he could recommend me for the driver corp, if I was interested. Hey, anything to keep me off my feet. I'm sure they've grown a full size since I've been here.

Friday, October 29, 1971

This morning we were issued with our dress uniforms, complete with dark red berets, white web belts, and gleaming leather boots (only the officers get to wear oxfords). No, there isn't going to be a dance! There's going to be a full dress parade on Monday. Of course we've already been instructed in proper parade deportment. Now I just have to clean and polish my rifle. We have a *dress rehearsal* tomorrow.

Saturday, October 30, 1971

Well, Diary, the *dress rehearsal* went off without a hitch. A Captain Crenshaw said that we made quite a polished company, notwithstanding the haranguing we'd received earlier from Sergeant Cumlings (difficult sod). He was probably ticked off that we got the rest of the day off from the usual grind. The boots, however, required yet another polishing, and the uniforms required brushing and pressing.

Monday, November 1, 1971

It could have been better, Diary. The rain absolutely pissed down! Talk about "raining on our parade." The fort commander, Colonel Gilcrist, along with Captain Crenshaw and their respective aides were under a tarp-roofed podium to take the salute, as we slogged smartly along in our gleaming boots and all. We all did a very smart "present arms" (if I say so myself) and Sergeant Cumlings gave the salute. That was one of the *high points* for us, seeing the sergeant getting drenched as well. Then we spent the rest of the day cleaning all the muck off our kit.

Tuesday, November 2, 1971

This morning at 0230 hours we were all rousted out of sound sleeps to *stand to* and prepare for a full kit scramble in the crisp morning air. Thankfully it had stopped raining by then, but everything was still dripping. We got back, soaked, scratched, and bone weary at 0500 hours for roll call and inspection before "chow." The sergeant proclaimed us a sorry-looking mess and then retired to get cleaned up himself. I will say of the sergeant, no matter what crap he puts us through, he does go through the thick of it with us. Well, that's something, I suppose.

Sunday, November 7, 1971

Well, Diary, the rest of this week was interspersed with "running the course," early morning, full kit rambles in the hillsides and range practice. I guess we must be getting tougher, though, because no one is dropping off in chapel anymore. I've gained almost twenty pounds, and I'm sure it must be muscle, because there's no way you could pack on fat here, although we are well fed.

Monday, November 8, 1971

I was given a crash course in a 6X6 PTV (personnel transport vehicle) today. It took some time before I got onto the gears, but once that was mastered, it didn't go too badly, according to Corporal Belkins (I think he's *game for my frame*!). However, if I was bounced into the roof once, I was bounced into it a dozen times (Thank God for the *tin pot* on my head). A smooth rider it's not. I'd feel sorry for the poor sods that would have to ride in the back.

Tuesday, November 9, 1971

Out in the 6X6 again today. Whatever happened to that nice little Jeep? The corporal asked me if I'd ever considered the tank corps. I'm not sure if he was casting aspersions on my driving skills or not. Anyway, if I was given the choice, I think I'd pass. I'd like to be able to see where I'm going through more than three inch by eight inch slots, thank you very much. Also, apparently, tanks aren't all that impervious to rocket fire.

Wednesday, November 10, 1971

The camp's all a-buzz with the upcoming passing out of recruits next Monday. Lists will be posted tomorrow with the names of those who have special qualifications. I'm hoping for a driver's spot. Corporal Belkins seems optimistic for me. Sergeant Cumlings wouldn't give me the slightest hint. To take our minds off it all, we were issued with our first combat uniforms today (no more khaki pyjamas!). Then we were divided into red and blue squads and went on battle manoeuvres. Finally, at 2100 hours, our red group managed to capture the blue flag. It was a difficult exercise because everyone, having been trained the same, naturally thought the same. Consequently, there were many mock casualties on both sides.

Thursday, November 11, 1971

This morning we had a special, multi-denominational and quite moving service for Veterans Day. Then, after chow, we did situation combat in a mock-up village. The sergeant overheard someone refer to it as "cowboys and Indians." The culprit was given the requisite tongue lashing and a hundred push-ups for his impertinence.

Friday, November 12, 1971

The buzz is still going about who's going to get what at passing out ceremony. This morning we did more range practice. Then we were issued with blank ammo and went on another battle manoeuvre. This time the blue squad captured the red squad's flag, but it took them longer. We didn't get back to barracks until almost midnight. However, there were fewer casualties, and the sergeant proclaimed that as a sign of improvement for a couple of squads of mental defectives, which seemed downright thoughtful of him.

Saturday, November 13, 1971

After morning chow, there was a surprise scramble that called for battle manoeuvres. This one ended in a close call, but the red captured the blue flag in less than four hours and with only three casualties. Sergeant Cumlings was so impressed that he invited both squads back to the NCO's mess for beer. I think he might be human after all.

Sunday, November 14, 1971

After chapel, we spent the rest of the day doing the spit-and-polish routine. The dress boots gleamed; the combat boots looked like new again; you could practically shave with the pressed creases in our dress uniforms; and our newly sewn-on cap badges and shoulder patches looked very impressive. Our rifles and side arms shone, inside and out. Extra care was taken with them because it was thought very unlikely that they would be fired again until actual combat. I even think that *Mother* Cumlings (as the sergeant was now discreetly called) was impressed.

Monday, November 15, 1971

Well, Diary, the big day has finally arrived! I don't think many of us got much sleep last night, judging by the eye-bags that most of us carried. After the usual morning callisthenics and chow, we retired to the barracks to get *dickied up* for parade at 1000 hours. I wonder if the term *dickey-up* is connected with the dickey that is worn under the uniform blouse, or jacket as civilians know them? Anyway, at 0930 hours, the sergeant assembled us in the barracks yard and marched us to the parade ground to the loud speakered strains of *The Stars and Stripes Forever.* There, we stood at ease for what seemed an eternity. Then, as the last note of *America the Beautiful* died away, Colonel Gilcrist and Captain Crenshaw, along with their two aides, mounted to the podium that was now bathed in sun shining from a cloudless sky. Sergeant Cumlings called us to attention, then to present arms, and then at ease. We all snapped to spectacularly, I thought. The roll was called by an aide, and after each name, the other aide said, "Congratulations!", which, of course, meant that the person was being passed out. Not one of the eighty-four recruits had flunked out. Afterwards, we assembled in the main hall and were given our "dog tags," regimental assignments and whatever commendations there were for outstanding performances. To my surprise, mine was for marksmanship. I was recommended as sniper material.

Well, I'd be off my feet alright, but possibly up a tree (a gum tree?) and not in a vehicle. A sniper's life expectancy in combat is apparently not that impressive. The sergeant, in his own inimitable way, made it absolutely clear the decision was final and there would not be an appeal made to the colonel. So, that was that, then; I would be coming back in a flag-shrouded metal box.

CHAPTER 6

As I looked back on those six weeks of boot camp from the rose-tinted vantage point of the distant future, it seemed to me that they had just flown by. I have to say that most of the *skills* that I had picked up at Fort Bragg in those six weeks actually did turn out to be useful. One or two of them may even have saved my life. But the camaraderie was, by far, the most outstanding thing in my mind. Some of the friends that I had made at boot camp and afterwards, in Vietnam and Cambodia, lasted at least till our official discharges. Sadly, many others that I got to know were no longer with us, including several Canadians.

It was only after passing out of boot camp that I could smile, at least inwardly, at some of Sergeant Cumlings' abrasive attempts at instilling discipline in his recruits. As though it would have been necessary after "bugle blare," he would roust us out of what was left of a sound slumber every morning, barring none (except for "scrambles," and those could've been at any time). His *good morning* tirade would unfailingly begin at 0600 with expletives referring to our questionable parentage, lowly position in the insect hierarchy, and with the always favourite: "Slap those warm, soft feet on that cold, hard floor and let's see some remote semblance of activity, you snivelling, mouth breathing maggots." (Can maggots really snivel?)

Oh, Cumlings was a charmer!

Although I didn't know it at the time, I would not have any further opportunity of keeping up what I facetiously referred to as my *diary* as I had planned at the outset. For one thing, field security unaccountably forbade it. I suppose they thought the enemy might inexplicably be able to make some sense of the vacuous drivel and the largely disjointed scratchings contained in most of such journals, and then use it against America in some undisclosed, devious, and dastardly fashion.

Anyway, after passing out ceremonies, we were all given a most welcomed seven days leave. Some hopped airlifts south to San Francisco or east to Reno to party. For some reason known only to the military brass, Los Angeles and Las Vegas were designated as out of bounds to us. Some others went home for maybe the last time in three years, and others surely for the last time altogether. Two other Canadians and I opted for quieter times and hitched a ride a few miles or so down the road to the Pacific coast.

The rugged beauty of that northern California coast line was just incredibly spectacular. It was far different than the common notion of Californian scenery that one might get from travel brochures or the movies, and it provided the perfect setting for some quiet time for introspection and for coming to terms with our immediate futures.

The salt scented breeze that blew off the steel grey, sky-domed Pacific seemed like the breath of freedom to us. How much longer would that freedom endure for the rest of the free world if the Communists had their way in South East Asia, I wondered? I was certain that this question had to be uppermost in the minds of many Americans. I just *had* to be certain of that, otherwise what was I doing here, and why had I undertaken to embark on this venture?

As we marvelled at the sights of dolphins cavorting in the surf and sea lions basking on the rocks, we talked of our hopes and dreams and of our fears and doubts—oh, there are always fears and doubts. We talked of our families and their various attitudes to it all. Perhaps oddly, there was no talk of girlfriends or sex. Then we would just drink beer and enjoy each other's silences for awhile as we merely gazed out to sea, sometimes unseeing and lost in our own thoughts—some perhaps of girlfriends and sex.

I was an only child and my decision to join up had been something of a disappointment and worry to my parents, not the least because I happened to join the *Yankee* military, not to mention that I would most likely be putting myself in some peril by going to Vietnam. They didn't seem to understand why I felt as I did about the American involvement and situation in Southeast Asia, or why I felt that I needed to be involved myself. As Dad had said: *What could* you *possibly do?*

It was none of our business was their view. *They had gotten themselves involved; let the American people see it through.*

My parents and so many others could not seem to appreciate that the boundary between our two countries could not refute the fact that we were all virtual family: brothers and sisters of the same continent. We had a common heritage. Whatever impacted one must surely impact the other. I felt that, in wartime or otherwise, we had an unwritten duty to one another; an enemy of the one was quite naturally an enemy of the other.

Anyway, because of what my parents knew I believed, I didn't feel very comfortable going back home for a farewell I knew would very likely be acrimonious, or at the very least uncomfortably strained. Instead, I wrote to my parents to say my farewells and to reaffirm my views and feelings in a last ditch hope that they may at least *try* and understand. I told them I'd write to them again when I could, and left it at that.

That might be construed by some as a cowardly way for a soldier to act. I preferred, rightly or wrongly, to think of it as an act of self-preservation. I didn't need to be taking any more angst into an anticipated battle zone than necessary.

The week of leave slipped by with amazing speed. When I thought about that apparent speed, for some reason I was reminded of Einstein's theory of the elasticity of time. Although I can't begin to understand quantum physics, the flight of that final week of freedom certainly seemed to confirm the theory. I only hoped that the speed of my eleven month tour of duty in Vietnam would comply with it as well.

It wasn't that I was having second thoughts; it was merely that I knew what was coming was, very likely, not going to be a romp in the park. In a strange way, I was actually looking forward to it—or at least to *my* involvement in an action that I may have some small part in bringing to a successful conclusion. A hubristic view of my possible contribution perhaps, but it was more of a hope that I might finally be a part of something positive and worthwhile. Anyway, I was to find out soon enough what my role was to be.

When we got back to base we were given twenty-four hours to say whatever farewells needed to be said and tend to whatever last minute preparations there were before debarkation at 0800 hours on the twenty-third of November.

I *bit the bullet* and took that opportunity to phone my parents, on the American taxpayer's dime, to tell them that I would be leaving shortly, to wish them well, and to try and not worry about me.

Fortunately, Dad wasn't home to reiterate his verbal vitriol at my perceived foolishness. He had been called back to work for yet more overtime. Mom simply told me she loved me, wished me well, and asked me to write whenever I could manage it.

It wasn't without a lump in my throat that I terminated that phone call. However, I forced myself to snap out of it and finished my preparations for debarkation.

Then, we would take a gruelling twenty hour flight from San Francisco to Clark Air Base in the Philippines, punctuated only by a refuelling stop in Hawaii. Catching up on sleep was virtually the only pastime on that flight. Then, a day and a half by supply ship across the dicey South China Sea to Vietnam (Phan Thiet to be exact). There was little, if any, sleep on that leg of the trip. From there, we endured a sweltering, dusty, bus ride to our new, temporary home at Tan Son Nhut—Bien Hoa, a military complex just outside of Saigon.

I was far too wiped by time lag and the humid heat of the place to take much of an interest in the *scenery* on the way there. I can just say that what I did notice of the *scenery* didn't impress me overly well. Then again, I wasn't really there to be impressed, one way or another, by the scenery at all. I was hardly a tourist.

The best that I can possibly say of it was that it was far different than anything I had ever seen (or smelled) before. Even so many years later, when I think about that first day, I can still conjure up the memory of that unique odour. It seemed to be an amalgam of sweating vegetation, sweating humanity, dust, and other things beyond the grasp of simple identification—though also not particularly pleasant.

Shortly after our arrival and when we had settled in, we were issued our assignments. To my considerable surprise, I had been given the provisional rank of Corporal SP-4. From what I could understand, it was somehow because of my designation as a marksman. Perhaps it was meant as an incentive of sorts. However, if it was an incentive of sorts, it didn't go so far as to be reflected in an increase in my pay rate. That would remain at E-2, or just over a hundred dollars a month paid in scrip and *not* U.S. dollars.

Apparently U.S. dollars were a big commodity on the *black market* in Vietnam. Some of the local (and illegal) currency dealers would pay as much as two or three scrip dollars for an American dollar. I'd even heard of isolated cases where the old "green back" went for as much as five scrip dollars. The Vietnamese piaster had all but gone out of general circulation as it had been rendered virtually without value. It wasn't uncommon to see wads of paper piasters used as insoles for leaking shoes.

CHAPTER 7

Almost from the first day of my arrival in South Vietnam, I became aware of some unusually extensive military withdrawals and administrative personnel evacuations being carried out. I thought it unaccountably odd. When I discreetly asked around, I was told by some of the *second hitchers* that it was only the non-essential civilian personnel that were being repatriated. Any military personnel that went with them were apparently only for security detail.

That seemed almost impossible to swallow. Why would security on that scale be so necessary if civilians were getting *away* from the area? It also didn't seem to answer the question of why so many of the withdrawing military personnel were high-ranking officers, amongst whom were several generals.

Our resident cynic and a boot camp buddy of mine, Stephen Whately, had his own particular take on it all, as usual.

"Christ, man, don't you see what's going down here? We've lost this sabre rattling contest, man, and the big wigs are scrambling to save their own overstuffed butts before the shit from the north hits the fan. As to the civvies, man, a lot of them are cute stenos and such and the generals are just taking their *squeezes* with them, man."

As ludicrous as that sounded to me, it seemed to make a good deal more sense than the initial explanation from those who maybe should have known.

What really puzzled me, though, was if the first part of what Whately said had any semblance of accuracy to it, why were they still training and sending troops over? There was certainly attrition happening: wounded and dead out, fresh *meat* in, but still . . .

Oh well, I thought, and to paraphrase Scarlett O'Hara: *I'll think about that tomorrow.*

But the questions could not so easily be put off.

By the time I left Vietnam, the highest ranking officers left, that I was aware of, were a half dozen full colonels and a brigadier general who flew in occasionally from the Philippines, where he apparently had his own cozy little beach front chalet overlooking Tayaba Bay.

CHAPTER 8

For the first ten days of my tour, I was sent north with some other newcomers, or FNGs, from various platoons to serve in observation and sentry duty along the demilitarised zone (DMZ). They needed a designated sniper, and I was *it*.

We newcomers were fondly tagged as *FNG* (Fucking New Guys) by the so-called *veterans*—those into their second hitch.

The DMZ was basically supposed to be a *no fire zone* for five kilometres on either side of the Ben Hai River that represented the geographic border between North and South Vietnam. The DMZ had been established as such since 1954 as a result of French involvement during their disastrous tenure here. We had every reason to feel relatively safe even though we had all heard of Vinh Moc where all hell could break loose anytime, from either side and, unaccountably, without fear of *official* repercussions, short of ineffectual grumblings, from such entities as the U.N. Security Council.

We were each issued with detailed maps of the area, a compass (way before the day of the GPS), binoculars, detailed instructions on engagement (if it should come to that), and the usual personal arsenal of an M16 rifle, a .45 calibre semi-auto side arm, a K-bar combat knife, a grenade sling, and ammo belts. Anything else we might need was stored at the post station bunker.

As the designated marksman, in place of the M16, I was issued with a semi-auto, day/night-scoped and flash shrouded .30-06 calibre sniper rifle complete with a thousand rounds of ammo. It was quite the weapon, with adjustable cheek and butt pads on its sinister looking matte black synthetic stock with a folding, adjustable bi-pod and black anodised stainless steel barrel. It would have been a deer hunter's dream, except that I wasn't going to be hunting deer with it. I was possibly going to have to shoot someone and that certainly gave me plenty of food for thought.

I did wonder about my sniper duty in that particular setting. The rifle, though a marvellous weapon, hardly had a ten kilometre range; and *a thousand rounds*? Did somebody know something that they weren't passing on? Somehow, I don't think that would have surprised me a great deal.

We were told that there hadn't been too much happening in our area of the DMZ for quite awhile, so the brass probably thought that it would be a bit of an easy exercise in acclimatization to our new environment. Most of us young grunts (FNG's) thought that it was a great idea. We'd play a little cards, catch up on letter writing, have some good bullshit sessions, maybe the odd game of football or baseball, and so on—almost like R and R leave. What could possibly go wrong?

So much for that thought. As it turned out, we had inadvertently been thrown in at the *deep end.* I had kind of wondered that if it was supposed to be so bloody peaceful, why all the damned hardware.

The proverbial shit hit the fan with a determined vengeance almost as soon as we arrived in Bo-Ho Su, just south of the river. The three H-19D "Chickasaw" choppers that we flew in on were just barely able to lift off with their return load of human cargo before all hell broke loose.

We hardly had time to stow our gear and get set up before 81mm mortar fire started landing just across the line. I didn't even have time to scramble up a sixty foot ladder into my armour-plated reconnaissance tower—not that I would have felt particularly comfy up there, given the activity. As it was, I just had enough time to dive unceremoniously into a sand-bagged enclosure with some of the others.

At first I thought that it must be some kind of impromptu drill. But no, it was just too damned realistic for that; and *real* was exactly what it turned out to be.

It wasn't until what proved to be a fifteen minute respite, that I was able to clamber, in what I felt was a most undignified manner, up into my recon tower with the help of a little covering fire. I'm still not absolutely certain that I didn't hear some Oriental sniggering coming from across the line.

I was told later that those breaks in barrages were just the enemy's attempt at a psychological ploy to try and unnerve us. My novice's impression was that these *ploys* were pretty damned effective.

One of my duties as a sniper on this particular campaign was to scope the surrounding area for possible enemy infiltration and to radio the locations back to the local operations headquarters (HQ). Also, I was to snipe (*snuff 'em* was the actual term used) whatever of those infiltrators that I could from my elevated vantage point. All that from what I considered a highly precarious position in my tin can perch.

In that circular, elevated enclosure, there was just room enough for one man, a couple of boxes of ammunition, and swinging room for a rifle. There was an eight inch high continuous spotting slot, with bullet deflectors, just below eye level around the perimeter. The armour plating was a quarter inch thick, so the occupant certainly didn't want an enemy's bullet to find its way into the enclosure to ricochet around until its energy was spent, or until it found a nice, fleshy target to embed itself in and put an end to its wayward travels. Below the spotting slot was a continuous shelf to rest the rifle's bi-pod on. Entrance was gained through a trap door in the floor. Homey it wasn't and the occupant certainly didn't want to be suffering from claustrophobia. Also, on a hot day, like most of them were, you couldn't spend more than an hour or so in that cooker, never mind that you had a good supply of water and salt tablets.

The NVA or VC or whoever the hell it was that was ruining our day must have been fairly close to use mortars. They certainly weren't bloody well *ten kilometres* away, but damned if I could see any sign of them no matter how carefully I scoped the area from which the mortars must obviously have been firing. I certainly had to hand it to them—they knew how to camouflage themselves. We could only hazard a very rough guess as to where they might be dug in by the direction from which the mortar fire was coming, but none of our return fire seemed to have the slightest effect on the onslaught.

The Army Bird Dogs that had been flying observation sorties over the area were unarmed and of no use to us in the circumstances. They merely, and very judiciously I thought, headed south at the first sign of trouble. We just hoped that they would at least radio our predicament to an appropriate source of assistance.

The mortar bombardment was soon joined by RPG (Rocket Propelled Grenades) and machine gun cover fire and kept up, off and on, for what seemed like an interminable length of time. It sounded like a snare drum tattoo was being played all around me. We mostly just kept our heads down and hoped for the best. I'm sure that more than a few of us just hoped that they would simply get fed up with their little game and go away and bug someone else. There wasn't much else we could do until some form of backup arrived or they ran out of ammo. At that point, I was just hoping that the former event would happen first.

This all continued for almost eighteen hours before the requested air assistance finally made a show. I guess the brass at the base couldn't quite believe we were having that kind of problem on our side of the DMZ; although, unknown to most of the newcomers, it had already happened several times in other areas along the DMZ. Apparently we didn't need to be made privy to that inconsequential tidbit of intelligence.

Once the 105's started their strafing runs it gave us enough respite to pop a few canisters of napalm in the enemy's general direction. By that stage of the Vietnam conflict, the use of napalm had *officially* been severely restricted. However, soon after we employed it, the enemy offensive melted away as though it had never been there at all, so we couldn't help feeling justified in thinking: *screw the officials*. In any case, napalm simply terrified them; I suppose with good reason because napalm was terrifying stuff with devastating effects on human flesh.

It was almost as though our resolve and readiness were being tested. But Christ, on our side of the water!

The following dawn, when we had the peace and quiet to do so, we scanned the area more thoroughly. Firstly, we scanned by glass, and then ever so gingerly, with mine detectors while on foot, and nervously braced every step of the way for a resumption of hostilities. That was the only time that I was pleased to remain in my elevated, stuffy tin can, and scan from the relative security that it provided.

Immediately over the south side of the demarcation line between the north and the south, the rest of the squad came across the places where the NVA (it actually did turn out to have been the NVA—they had left some of their easily identifiable gear) had secreted themselves. In spite of the trauma their attack had caused, I couldn't help but admire their cunning and industriousness. They may well have been piss poor shots, but they were surely cunning and industrious.

The area that they had fired from was every bit as barren as a moonscape with absolutely no place on the surface to hide. What they had managed to do, however, was to dig three tunnels, from somewhere farther north, to within about two hundred yards of the south side of the demarcation line on our bloody side of the river. The balls of these buggers! Then they had dug upwards and created camouflaged pits over each tunnel so their mortars were just below our eye level and virtually invisible from our perspective.

They had done all of that from the cramped shelter of the tunnels, presumably at night, but under the very noses of the sentries patrolling on our side of the line. There was no doubt in my mind that some embarrassing questions would be asked about that lapse in security. Then they would have had to drag all the excavated earth back through the tunnels to dispose of it at the starting point. The project must have taken them weeks. How and where the hell had they crossed the river undetected? And how the hell had they managed to get through the land mines speckled all over our side of the river bank? All that while carting their mortars, shells and other arms and ammunition with them? Oh yes, questions would be asked.

All of that labour for a one-off assault! They were certainly industrious, if nothing else. I couldn't help but be reminded of an army of ants. Well, it was said they had an ant colony mentality after all, and that particular endeavour surely seemed to verify that assertion.

Although I thought it was all very ingenious, I was smart enough to keep my opinion to myself. After all, they'd had the unwitting help of some rather sloppy sentry protocol. Also, all of the newcomers especially had been more than a little shaken by the whole sudden onslaught and might not appreciate my *traitorous* view.

Even though there had been no major injuries and, thankfully, no casualties, it all really rattled us pretty well, I can tell you. Constipation certainly wasn't a common complaint.

We collected a few NVA mementos for posterity before destroying as much of the tunnels as we could with a few pats of plastique explosive. Then we just called it a day.

The rest of the time we spent there, before we were relieved to make our way back south, was eerily uneventful, given the hectic activity of the first day. It was so uneventful that some even started joking about "the day the sky fell." However, I still kept my reluctant admiration of the enemy to myself—my momma hadn't raised any fools.

The blasé attitude was only on the surface, though. There weren't any serious bullshit sessions and not much by way of card playing. There were only a few letters written and certainly no impromptu football or baseball games played out in the open. There was the odd poker game with NVA memorabilia at stake, but nobody really seemed all that relaxed until we were finally on our way back.

When we got back to base, there was the usual debriefing exercise. That's when some potentially embarrassing questions were asked regarding security protocol. However, it was eventually and grudgingly deemed that our group was blameless. The brass seemed disappointed when they couldn't attach blame somewhere. Then we just sat around to await our next *gig*.

As it would turn out, that would be my one and only brush with anything remotely resembling real combat. Things certainly didn't get better, though.

The following are just a few of the dazzling array of aircraft that saw service during the Vietnam conflict years

The Bird Dog was employed primarily for surveillance and low level reconnaissance.

This little "workhorse", the Cessna O-2 Skymaster, was also employed in surveillance and low level reconnaissance.

This "chopper", the Sikorsky H-19B Chickasaw, was employed throughout as a troop deployment vehicle as well as for rescue.

This aging, heavily armed fighter/bomber, the Republic F-105D, first saw active Cold War defence duty in 1958 over the then West Germany. In Vietnam it saw effective action as a fighter as well as a light bomber.

The Bell Huey HH-H1 served practically throughout the conflict as a medical evacuation and rescue vehicle.

Another particular "workhorse", the HU-16B Albatross, saw fairly extensive service over and around the South China Sea in the field of troop, supplies and equipment deployment.

Another aging aircraft, the Douglas C-124 Globemaster II (nicknamed Old Shaky) saw fairly extensive service as a troop and cargo transport vehicle.

The Piaseckie H-21 Shawnee also saw service as a troop and equipment transport vehicle for the Army.

The fairly heavily armed Sikorsky HH-3 (fondly referred to as the Jolly Green Giant) saw extensive service as an attack helicopter, although it also performed some rescue duties.

This formidable looking monster, the Lockheed RB-69A, saw extensive action as a high altitude, long range, special operations reconnaissance aircraft.

CHAPTER 9

One of the highlights of what might otherwise have been a monotonous day around base camp was provided by something we called *Radio Vietnam*. It was comprised of an assortment of broadcasts on both AM and FM radio as well as television by the American Forces Vietnam Network (AFVN). Their slogan was: *Serving the American fighting men twenty-four hours a day from the Delta to the DMZ*—and they certainly fulfilled that admirably.

They'd had more than their fair share of problems, however. Dissidents from the National Front for the Liberation of Vietnam, a ragtag assortment of northern, Commie sympathisers and members of the Pathet Lao had, over a period of years, tried to shut them down, or at least severely hamper their efforts at morale building. They had tried to accomplish that with bombings and various other means of sabotage. It had been the first time I'd ever even heard of a "car bomb." However, quite a number of the original installations were still in existence and pounding out their music and messages almost up to the end of the conflict in 1975.

One of the more or less *cushy* jobs would be getting assigned to security duty at a radio or television installation. That *cream pie* assignment, though, was usually given to those who had just returned from some particularly nasty mission or other; almost a form of R and R. Unfortunately, I was never afforded the opportunity. That was really too bad because I would have found it very interesting to be able to *nose* around a broadcast facility. I had become very intrigued by radio broadcasting while listening to the broadcasts of shipboard pirate radio stations in and around Britain and continental Europe while travelling there in the mid-sixties.

Wherever we would go in camp, there would always be a radio or television set going, and we could hear such memorable programmes as *Good Morning Vietnam*, later of movie fame and greatly altered by Robin Williams. Other programmes included such favourites as Dawnbuster, Nightbeat, Sergeant Pepper, Million Dollar Music, Soul Train, Orient Express, Town and Country, Panorama, and the ever popular Top 30 Countdown.

There would be messages from home for birthdays or other special occasions, and always a great variety of up to date music in whatever genre anyone could appreciate. Also, news that kept us in touch with what was happening elsewhere in the world was a special favourite with some. Others didn't seem to give a shit about anything but getting back home in one piece and as soon as possible. Of course, in all realms of human endeavour, there are always those who are only where they are because they feel that they don't have any other viable option.

Also, in the circumstances, there was the virtually inevitable political propaganda side to some of the broadcasts, especially on T.V., and especially in the early years. I guess it must have been felt that we had to be spoon fed what we *needed* to know to operate effectively. Later, the propaganda couldn't compete with the obvious facts that everyone, who had spent any length of time in Vietnam, knew only too well, so it was largely curtailed. However, what there was left of it lasted almost to the end as well. Even in that setting, there was always the odd, gullible dreamer amongst us. Ah, the innate optimism of the human spirit . . .

All things considered, though, it was certainly a great morale booster, in all but one respect, that is. That one respect, of course, was the somewhat demoralising and unaccountable broadcasts of the toll of those reported missing in action and a body count that went on every day. Every week, day by day, almost hour by hour it mounted, and for some unknown reason it was felt that we should be made aware of it all. Perhaps it was thought that it might somehow spur us on to greater effort, who knows.

Those announcements alongside the propaganda about how great we were doing seemed to me to mix as well as oil and water.

That was the only *downer* of the whole performance. None of us would have missed the rest of the broadcasts, though, if we could have helped it. For the most part, it certainly proved to be a great diversion for the administration corps and those bored service men and women awaiting a mission. It was right up there, second only to receiving the ever welcome letters and parcels from home.

By 1972 the seven AFVN detachments had closed. The AFVN was renamed the American Radio Service in 1973, and radio service was scaled back to only one FM station in the Saigon area. The AFVN staffers from the former detachments helped Vietnamese technicians to improve the South Vietnamese television and radio services (THVN).

Can Tho Channel 78 (UHF) T.V. and retransmitted AFVN—T.V. Channel 11 Saigon, with Bob Morecock and Jerry Elliot, were still received in the Mekong Delta area along with various other local AM and FM radio stations.

The battle to boost morale still went on right up to the bitter end, and, at least in my opinion, it is not possible to heap too many glowing accolades on the radio and T.V. staffers and broadcasters of the AFVN.

CHAPTER 10

Although it wasn't common knowledge amongst most of the lower ranked service personnel, for some time there had been general preparations for a withdrawal from the *theatre of operations*—in military parlance. An important part of that thrust included bringing in troops from areas that were no longer deemed to be viable operations. Some of those troops had been listed as missing in action (MIA), and as it would be a face saving gesture for the government to redeem as many of those as possible before the final withdrawal, search and repatriation (S and R) operations had been implemented.

My next assignment was with a non-combat search and repatriation company that consisted of four platoons (about a hundred and twenty men). It was all quite "hush-hush," or as hush-hush as anything like that could possibly be at the time and in the circumstances.

Apparently there were some troops who had been listed as *missing* (MIA). They all needed to be found for evacuation and eventual debriefing, if they were still alive. If they were deceased, their position was to be recorded for *possible* retrieval.

Each platoon was split into three groups, simply designated as A, B and C, and each group would have one field medic and one or two "old timers" along who apparently knew the terrain for the area of that group's particular S and R operation.

As a non-combat unit, we were each issued only with refurbished, World War II M1A1 .30 calibre semi auto carbines (which more than a few of us thought a bit odd if not downright tacky), each with two—twenty round banana clips and two-ten round box clips, a .45 calibre Government Colt side arm with five-seven round clips, a K-bar combat knife and a machete. *All for self defence only*.

I must admit to being somewhat put out that a *classified marksman*, such as myself, should be reduced to carrying a combat rifle that must have been at least as old as I was. But there you have it: *the military way*.

I was more than slightly surprised to find out that some of the missing were reportedly just across the line into Cambodia and that's where we, Owl Platoon, would be headed. What the hell had the marines been doing in Cambodia? No wonder these S and R missions were supposed to be hush-hush, even given the U.S. invasion back in April of 1970.

For this they needed a marksman? Go figure.

We were forbidden to take anything with us that could possibly identify us or our military attachment: photos, letters from home, wallets, even dog tags. A strip search before we left made sure of our compliance. (A strip search, for Christ sake!) They were certainly serious about our anonymity. All this, of course and including the outdated rifles, was deemed necessary in the event we were captured. Oh, wonderful! Someone had mused that it was surprising that we weren't just given clubs and rawhide shields and were made to dress in skin loincloths.

I remember wondering if it was possible that they thought for a minute we could pass ourselves off as tourists, perhaps. Also, I couldn't help but wonder if that enforced anonymity in those circumstances wasn't in violation of some convention or other.

Even after such a short time with dog tags around my neck, I felt almost naked, and even slightly vulnerable, without them. Oddly, I felt that it was somewhat like wearing a ski mask in a bank. I wasn't at all comfortable with the forced anonymity, and also had to wonder how we would ever be identified by our own side if the worst came to the worst.

We were D Company, Fourth Battalion attached to the Twenty-third Army Infantry Regiment, Fifth Division; and we were headed into basically forbidden territory on a ten day mission to locate and evacuate four lost marines, or at least bring back their dog tags and the exact coordinates of their bodies—and all of that with minimal and antiquated fire power.

What the hell had I gotten myself into!

CHAPTER 11

After we had been briefed, and a couple of days before we were to embark on our S and R mission, our platoon was given a twelve hour leave. Some of us decided that it might be a blast to make for the heady climes of Saigon and partake of whatever treats it may have to offer "shave tails" from States side. We were each given a package of a dozen government-issue condoms (just in case we got really *busy*), a street map, our first pay packet of scrip currency (with the tongue-in-cheek admonition not to spend it all in one place), and sent on our way in the backs of a couple of PTVs.

The ride was monotonously uneventful, though damned rough even on the paved part of the road, which seemed to sport more than its fair share of pot holes. I would more than gladly have traded places with the driver. I felt it should have been my job in any case.

From our tarp-shrouded perches, what we could see of the views on the way certainly weren't anything to write home about either. By way of vegetation, there were only gnarled, stunted, and seared looking trees whose mostly leafless branches seemed to be lifted in prayer entreating the heavens for some semblance of moisture. There were sparsely spaced tufts of tall, equally seared looking grass whose reason for existence seemed highly questionable.

Over all this hung an almost continuous pall of dust swirled into dancing eddies by the passing traffic, of which there appeared to be a surprising abundance. Even the sky was an uninteresting light dun colour that matched, almost to perfection, the colour of the parched and cracked soil that looked to be staring disconsolately from between the sparse and withered tufts of flora.

As to the native fauna, there were only the odd dead, emaciated and mostly desiccated dogs in varying stages of decomposition lying at the sides of the road. Other apparent animals, all dead but beyond the stage of identification, also lay crumpled along the arid fringes. On that trip, nothing living presented itself at the sides of the road. Perhaps continued existence in that environment might not have been the better option for them.

As we approached the city, we could actually smell it almost ten minutes before we arrived. It was a distinctly strange odour to say the least. It seemed to comprise an odd comingling of the bestial and the natural, as though a breath of the blood, sweat, and excrement of generations rose from the very earth in an exhalation to create the very atmosphere of the place.

So this was the high life centre of South Vietnam!

As we climbed stiffly down from the vehicles, in what I soon realised was the edge of the "red light" district, we were immediately descended upon by a literal multitude of purveyors and vendors of everything imaginable from gaudy baubles and knick-knacks, to food and drink, to drugs of an amazing variety, and to "flesh" ranging in age from about twelve to approximately eighty by the look of them.

With regard to the "flesh market," the typically colourful sales banter would be something like: "Hey Joe, you want good time? She ruv you rong time. Good bang-bang. Ten dollah sclip. Eight dollah 'm'elican dollah. Come on, come on; you have good time, rong time. Rook, you make heh wet alleady. Hey come on, Joe, ten dollah cheap fo good time, rong time, you bet. Maybe you rike young boy mo betta? We got, velly nice, you see."

"By Christ, look at that one," quipped one of the *wags*, indicating a particularly ancient-looking and rather porcine specimen with wispy, sparse hair that stood in all directions as though the owner had just received a substantial electric shock .

"How the hell would you know which wrinkle to stick it in?"

"Why don't you just go and find out?" replied another.

"Christ, it would be like *doing* your granny, assuming that it *is* a woman," said yet another.

This was followed by a volley of raucous, knowing guffaws and shoulder punches. I couldn't help but think to myself: *Do your mommas know you're out and about?*

The sales banter for other commodities was only slightly less frenetic. On and on it went until the crush, babble and cloying and acrid scent of humanity became more than a little overwhelming.

We broke up into groups of three and four, clumsily accomplished our escape and began wandering the streets and lanes of the immediate area. A few of the more adventurous took almost immediate advantage of the wares offered by the *hooker hawkers*. A few others of us weren't quite so sanguine about coming away from such liaisons totally unscathed by some seriously debilitating scourge or other—even with the use of the government's precautionary aids. We few merely contented ourselves with bar entertainment, strip clubs, American beer, and local cuisine.

To the more adventurous gourmand, the food was really quite delicious, though few of us could have told you what most of it might have been. Very little of it actually resembled anything you might have found in an Oriental eatery in North America at that time.

Whether or not it had anything to do with our inability to identify most of what we ate, some of us later marvelled at the singularly scant cat and rat populations in the otherwise teeming, scavenger ridden alleys. I, for one, really didn't care to dwell on it too much.

On each side of the main strip of the district were hung garlands of coloured light bulbs (mostly red—apparently the Vietnamese colour for luck and prosperity). Interspersed with these were small American flags. As a matter of fact just about every window in the street sported at least one American flag. I suppose that was meant to help the "Joes" feel more at home and make them more inclined to spend their money. I guess the poor buggers thought that they might as well make as much money as they could while they could. I think that most of them could almost feel the end nearing. At that point, they certainly felt more than I did. They may have been living almost like animals, but they weren't necessarily stupid.

Something not quite so inviting and "homey" was the air of the place. It was redolent with the mingled odours of opium, urine, pot, cooked fish, and something else that I couldn't quite put my finger on—not that I would have been inclined to, my innate curiosity notwithstanding.

Anyway and all in all, everyone seemed to have had a marvellous time, as could have been witnessed by the more than ample display of gaudy baubles and knick-knacks bought for the girlfriends and other loved ones back home, the good humoured ribaldry, fantastic stories of vaunting sexual prowess, and projectile vomiting into the gutters after a drinking binge of Bacchanalian proportions.

The festivities all came to a halt when we were picked up (literally, in some cases) at 0200 and all tumbled into our beds about an hour later. I think we had all of about three hours of sleep, or some other form of unconsciousness, before the loud-speakered "bugle blare" at 0600.

That morning, when most of the previous evening's celebrants were once again clear headed enough to understand the spoken word, we were given a review of our original briefing. Then those who required it set to medicating splitting headaches and the accompanying photophobia as well as last minute preparations for embarkation the following day at 0700.

CHAPTER 12

"You knew about this, for Christ's sake!" I said to Stephen Whately, my fellow boot camp buddy, "and never thought to tell your old bud, here?"

"Don't get your shit in a steam, man. I just guessed, okay? I thought it was damned funny about a couple of things and just put two and two together. That's all, man," he said.

"What things? Come on, let's have it, *man*. We've got all bloody day in this glorified river raft, *man*."

Pointedly pretending not to have noticed my very apparent slur on his virtually constant use of the word, *man*, almost as a form of punctuation, he continued: "Man, didn't you kinda notice that we were sort of *pushed* through basic training? And the fact that we only got a week off at the end of it all, man, instead of the usual thirty days' leave should have told you that someone was in a bloody big rush for something, man."

"I didn't give it much thought," I said, somewhat mollified, and masking the fact that I hadn't given it *any* thought at all. "I just figured that it was the *military way*, given that there have been some withdrawals going on because of the push for peace and all," I hedged.

"Oh man! So what the hell did you think we were coming over here for, man?"

I had no satisfactory answer for that, so we just fell into a mutually accepted silence and listened to the sounds from the jungle on both sides of us and the rumble of the boat engines. Although I realised that good old Stephen always gave the impression that he knew more than he really did, what he had said prompted me to think. Was I really that naïve? Or was I just so focussed on getting over here that I didn't think much about anything else?

Just what the hell else weren't we being told? And why not?

We were on what appeared to be a converted PT boat: a small gun boat of sorts that was completely unblemished by any military markings except for painted khaki, beige, and green camouflage on the hull. The khaki certainly matched the water of the Mekong to a tee. The boat had a large canvas sun and rain canopy over the back deck where ten of us from Owl Platoon, C group were scrunched down against the four foot high, armour-plated gunnels. A .50 calibre machine gun was mounted on each side. That and our own limited ordnance was our sole defence till we got to our debarkation point more than half way up the Mekong River towards Phnom Penh. To all intents and purposes we could have been *innocent* drug runners, for all a casual observer might know.

We were to be dropped off across the river from the village of Rieng Hong, but there was strictly no contact to be initiated with any of the locals. We would bivouac in the jungle overnight, then were to proceed inland and northward into Cambodia on the following morning.

Our group leader and field commander of Owl platoon was Master Sergeant Burt Gorman. He was a grizzled old Aussie warhorse who had been in the army since God had invented apples, and if anyone could bring us out of this alive, he could. He had said it was going to be a walk in the park. *That*, I wasn't too sure of, although he did generally instil confidence in all of his men.

Second in command and leader of C group was another old timer, Master Corporal William "Wilful" Phillips. Much against the wishes of his family, he'd given up a very promising career as an accountant with Chase Manhattan in New York to volunteer for a stint in Korea in '51. It was thought that that was very likely where he got the "Wilful" handle from, though he never said. As a matter of fact, he never said very much at all about his life in the "Big Apple", nor anything at all about why he had made such an abrupt and drastic career change. As usual, of course, speculation on the QT was rampant, and all amply coloured and generated by a combination of a certain amount of boredom and overactive imaginations. Someone had even offered the highly unlikely scenario that he had embezzled a "whack of dough" and was "hiding out" in the army. (Brazil would probably have been *my* first choice, but then, what do I know?)

Then there was the *kid* of the platoon, Private Thomas A. Wakefield. He was tagged by some with the handle of *Tom-tom.* I think he rather despised that particular nick name—not nearly *manly* enough, don't you know. He tried to pass himself off for eighteen and said that he'd joined up on his eighteenth birthday. Most of us who thought about it at all doubted that very much and were sure that his *real* birth certificate wouldn't have borne it out either. He was just a very nice kid trying too hard to be a man. Most of us tried to humour him and just hope that it wouldn't get him killed.

Almost everyone called Wakefield, *Kid*, which he didn't like much either, but it stuck anyway. He just called me, *Old Man*, partly because of his *posh* British background and partly because I was the third oldest man in the platoon and the only one he dared to call old man. We got along well, though, and had sort of adopted one another. I confess to have taken something of a protective attitude towards him; especially after he had confided to me that his middle initial stood for Asquith. *Asquith*, for Christ sake! Imagine any parents tagging a kid with a moniker like that—posh English or not.

The Kid had said that he hadn't wanted to become a *snotty* officer and had vehemently declined his family's offer to get him into West Point. He said that he'd much preferred to be an *on the ground grunt.* What he apparently lacked in common sense, he certainly seemed to make up for in pure guts. Maybe carrying around a middle name like *that* gave him the guts, or maybe it was just an uncertain bravado spurred on by ignorance.

"Hey, Old Man," the Kid said, snapping me out of my reverie, "would you care to try some of my Gran's homemade humbugs? They're really very good. You'll have to pry them apart, though, because they're all melted together with this blasted humidity."

I looked at his pale, sweat glistened face and smiled to myself as I realised that, humid as it was, the sweat was actually the result of being sea sick—*mal de mare* on the bloody river. I had always thought that all the British had seafaring embedded in their genetic makeup. Well, apparently not *all*.

"Sure," I said, but as I reached for the proffered brown paper bag, what turned out to be a mortar shell explosion off the port amidships rocked the boat and a shower of muddy water cascaded over the port gunnel.

The helmsman gave the engines full throttle as our port .50 cal. started spitting a reply. Our fire was in turn answered by small automatic arms fire from the jungle that extended to the river's edge.

When another explosion sent water cascading over the port stern, I looked around for the Kid. I spotted him curled in a foetal ball with his ass in the air and keening softly to himself.

A third explosion off to the stern rocked the boat yet again, and something that sounded for all the world like a loud, sharp "brap" issued from the ass of the Kid's pants. At first I thought that he'd somehow been hit. Then the sound was followed closely by the unmistakeable aroma of fresh, liquid excrement.

All fell silent then, except for Whately who exclaimed the obvious, "For Christ's sake, man, the Kid's shit himself!"

"Shut your flapping cake hole, asshole," barked the Sarge. "There's bugger all he can do about that now. He can clean up once we've landed. Is everyone okay?"

We all sounded off that we were fine, but the poor Kid would have to sit in his own shit for another two hours.

"Hey, Kid," I said, trying to lighten his embarrassment a bit, "where're those humbugs of your Gran's?"

The Kid smiled shamefacedly, squirmed into a sitting position, which couldn't have been all that comfortable in the circumstances, and passed me the bag that had been clutched in his sweating hand the whole time.

At least some of the colour seemed to have returned to his face, and the sweat had miraculously dried.

CHAPTER 13

Stephen Whately's dad was a big shot realtor who ran his own real estate company in Seattle and wanted his mainly shiftless boy to follow in his footsteps. Because his dad usually grossed upwards of a quarter million dollars a year, when that amount of money counted for something, Stephen gave it a half-hearted try for about six months. Then he told his dad that his heart just wasn't in it and he was going to quit. His dad countered with an ultimatum: either give it a serious try for at least two years, or get the hell out of the house and just *try* to make it on his own.

Incensed by what he thought of as his dad's blatant insensitivity, Stephen counter-countered by moving in with his girlfriend, Gloria van den Klaast, but Stephen just couldn't seem to dodge the ultimata. After two months of sponging on her, Gloria basically told him, in as lengthy and searing a tirade as she could muster, to get a job or get out.

What was the poor boy to do? Now he felt not only misunderstood but totally unloved as well; so, in the grip of illogical rebellion and muddled thinking, he hiked on down to the recruiting office and signed up.

Gloria was apoplectic. She told him that this act of lunacy was tantamount to attempting suicide, and if that's all he thought of her and their future together then he could bloody well go and *off* himself if he liked, and not to come crawling back to her with no arms or legs.

Well, I did say that she was apoplectic, didn't I.

After those body blows to his ego, poor old Stephen became despondent a lot of the time and fairly cynical the rest of the time. Well, it's little wonder, really. Gloria was a knock out gorgeous, leggy, lithesome blond who apparently was extremely acrobatic and inventive in the sack. The precipitous drop-kick into reality that she had laid on him was bound to have affected him adversely. I know—I've seen her photos and heard endless accounts of her libidinous bedroom activities—bedroom or apparently anywhere else, for that matter.

In the army most of the despondency was kicked out of him, but that only tended to increase the cynicism. Stephen Whately must surely be the only guy I knew who didn't mature much because of the ministrations and influences of the armed forces. He went in at twenty years old going on twelve and came out at twenty four going on just about thirteen.

Gloria apparently got over her violent disappointment because, after his military discharge, she and Stephen ended up getting married and living in a surprisingly sustained, if somewhat stormy, marital existence. It

was said that it wasn't known if she was making a
good wife, but she was certainly making him a good
husband. There was evidently a lot of truth in that
assertion, because Stephen eventually went back into
the real estate business and actually did extremely well
at it.

CHAPTER 14

"Is that a letter from *the boy* you're reading there?"

Dad had just come back from a double shift at the plant and noticed the buff, U.S. metre-stamped envelope on the kitchen table. Not too much got past the *old boy*.

"Yes, dear and *our son* seems to be doing well. He sounds quite enthusiastic about his role *over there*," she said, reluctant to use the name, Vietnam.

She had deliberately emphasized "our son." It was just her small way of showing defiance; and even that small gesture was daring for her.

"Yah, well, I guess nobody's started shooting at him yet. Give him a week over there and you can just bet that he'll be seeing the folly of his decision. Damned fool kid."

"Now dear, have a little charity for your own son. He really believes in what he's doing, you know, and I think it shows real character, whether we agree with him or not."

"Yah, and that *character*'ll do him a whole helluva lot of good if he comes back in a box."

"You do say the cruellest things sometimes," Mom said, fighting back the tears. "What about when you tried to sign up in the last war? If you'd made it, you could have come back in a box too, you know."

That last bit of Mom's uncharacteristic defiance succeeded in turning Dad's already ruddy complexion to a decidedly darker hue accompanied by dangerously pulsating veins in his temples.

"That was way different," he vented. "I wanted to go over there for *our* king and *our* country and *not* some bloody *foreign* country that should bloody well be minding their own goddamned business. Now there's an end of it," and he scowled as only Dad could whenever he was reminded of what he must have viewed as his shortcoming. "Now, what's for supper? I've been doing *real* work, you know."

The right way, the wrong way and Dad's way!

There was no mention, nor any apparent thought, of the fact that he was a married man when he tried to enlist and could have been leaving a pregnant wife to go off to a war thousands of miles away, and that I was unencumbered by any such considerations and responsibilities.

I was wrong and he was right, and never mind any inconsistencies in logic. Good old Dad!

When Mom related it all to me much later, I would like to have thought that his tirade was just his way of showing concern for me, but that was just too difficult a stretch for me to make, given the state of our past relationship.

I had blatantly chosen to ignore his directive, and that was just too much *insubordination* for him to bear.

For her own reasons, Mom certainly didn't agree with what I was doing, but at the very least she did agree with my sentiment in doing it. Sometimes I thought that she would have benefitted from a similar break from her husband, and then let *him* get on with what he euphemistically might like to call a life on his own.

CHAPTER 15

"Awright, you muckers, let's try and not leave any sign of our overnight picnic, shall we?" said the Sarge. "How you doin' there, Kid?"

"Fine, thanks, Sergeant," he replied. "Now that I'm on solid ground, I'll be good to go, sir."

"Well enjoy the solid ground while you can, Kid. It won't stay that way for long by the look of the sky."

And the sergeant was right.

We had only been hacking our way through the underbrush for a couple of hours when the heavens opened up. Although the jungle canopy was quite dense, we were all soaked to the skin in a matter of minutes, regardless of our ponchos. I've rarely seen a downpour to match it, even on the Canadian prairies, and it would last for most of the rest of the day.

Just after midday, and almost six hours of that slog, the sergeant signalled for a halt in a small clearing. We hastily strung up a tarp and collapsed under it.

After a cold chow of C rations, the sergeant sent Wilful and me to scout ahead.

"Keep your eyes open and your cake holes shut," he admonished. "There've been reports of some Khmer Rouge splinter groups roaming the area. We probably ran into some of the buggers downriver. There should be a large marshy meadow about a mile or so due west-north-west of here, but if you see or hear any sign of activity before then, you can just get your bloody sad asses back here, pronto. You still owe me fifty bucks, Wilful, and I'd like to be able to collect it in this lifetime."

"You know me, Sarge. I always pay my debts in a timely fashion." Wilful grinned broadly.

Then Wilful and I set off with a minimal load. After about two hours of beating our way through fairly dense jungle, we came to an abrupt end to it. I almost laughed out loud with sheer joy and relief at the sight of it. It was a large expanse of little else than marsh grass for two or three miles across.

We were both dog tired, and our wrists and fingers were almost twice their usual thicknesses from constantly swinging our machetes.

We crouched down at the edge of the marsh and carefully glassed the area across which we would have to go. Although the binoculars were constantly fogging up, we couldn't detect anything moving or out of the ordinary over that large, open expanse.

Then, as we were just about to head back, I spotted a dark shape back in the trees and across on the other side. Wilful confirmed that it looked like some kind of broken structure. Maybe it could afford us a bit of shelter for the coming night, we thought. If it was going to continue pissing down, and at that point it certainly looked as though it would, we would certainly be in need of a bit of shelter.

When we got back, we made our report to Sarge, rested up for about half an hour, and then all of us packed up and headed out once more. By this time, it was getting late and what little light there had been filtering through the trees was seriously starting to fail. However, we had no trouble following the trail that Wilful and I had hacked out, although I'm sure we all thought the trail could be a mixed blessing. If we could follow it so easily, so could *others*.

Just as we arrived at the edge of the marsh, the rain stopped as suddenly as it had started so many hours before. It was a bit eerie, just as though some giant hand had turned a tap off. The steady downpour, however, had done its work; the ground was like mush.

Before we ventured out onto the open marsh, we planted a few trip flares at the end of our trail just in case we might attract any curious visitors into tailing us.

As we walked through that sodden mire, the audible rhythm of our pace was almost hypnotic: "Shlock, shlock, shlock, shlock!" On and on it went for what seemed like an eternity.

Then, about half way across the marsh, from under my left foot came a distinct slurping sound followed closely by a "click" and "crunch", as though I'd stepped on dry twigs in a bowl of custard. But nothing in this bog was dry, though the ground did seem to have the consistency of fresh custard.

I froze on the spot. For an instant I thought that I may have stepped on an anti-personnel mine, but only for an instant. A body shattering explosion didn't take place, but suddenly there rose to my nostrils the most indescribably nauseating smell I had ever experienced. It enveloped me and seemed to soak into my very skin. It was a putrescence of such heavily cloying import that I thought I was going to retch on the spot.

The stench was vaguely reminiscent of one I experienced once when I came across the decaying, bloated carcass of a dead horse on a muggy August morning many years before.

"What the hell's the matter?" came Wilful's gruff whisper from behind, as he just about collided with me in the dim, cloud shrouded light of the moon.

I just couldn't muster an answer. I was literally paralysed into silent immobility, except for the churning sensation in my stomach.

Wilful grabbed my arm from behind and that seemed to break the trance. As the moon peered through a rift in the drifting clouds, I looked down and damn nearly upchucked what I'd had for my last several meals.

In the pale light of the moon I could clearly see what it had been that I'd stepped into. That vision would stay vividly with me for a good part of the rest of my life.

I had stepped into the body of a dead man—not metaphysically, but actually. Although I could only *assume* it might have been a man, I definitely *knew* he was dead: he was in a highly advanced state of decomposition and I stood ankle deep in what had once been his abdominal cavity. As I stared dumbly down at this apparition, I became aware of *things* wriggling and swarming over my boot.

That jolted me suddenly back to reality. I wrenched clear of Wilful's grasp and of the decomposing corpse, and bolted several steps ahead, shaking, stomping, and wiping my foot as I went to try and rid it of that awful, stinking infested gore. All that to the gleeful accompaniment of Wilful's muted laughter after he realised what had happened.

How the hell any of the others ahead of me had missed stepping into it remains a mystery to me to this day. Just my luck, I guess.

In retrospect, I have to admit that it must have been a damned amusing sight: a soldier in full kit doing a bloody jig by moonlight in the middle of a Cambodian marsh. However, the sergeant wasn't much amused—at least not at the time.

"What the fuck are you playing at, Corporal?" That was Sergeant Gorman's gruff whisper.

"He stepped into a dead gook and messed up his boots," came Wilful's obviously amused reply. "I think he'll be bunking on his own tonight, Sarge."

"Awright, assholes, if you've finished partying over the dead gook, is it okay if we get a move on before we find ourselves partying with *live* ones?" said Gorman.

The mirth vanished like mist in a gale.

At that particular time the sarge apparently didn't marvel much at my terpsichorean prowess either.

CHAPTER 16

We eventually arrived at the far side of the marsh, thankfully without further incident. It's amazing how tough and tiring it can become walking through tall marsh grass for any length of time. It wasn't wholly unlike wading through hip deep water.

Anyway, we found the structure that Wilful and I had spotted earlier. It appeared to be a large, derelict and ruined, corrugated metal storage shed of some kind. Although there seemed to be some evidence of burning, whether it had been ruined by explosion or the elements, we couldn't rightly tell by the inadequate light of the moon. However, even with half of the roof missing, it was shelter after a fashion.

We did wonder about what it could have been used for, who had built it and for what purpose, and why the hell way out in the *boonies*. There was some speculation of it perhaps having been a drug lord's warehouse, which seemed the most plausible explanation. That would certainly have accounted for the isolation of the place. However, as no one seemed to have a definitive explanation, we merely shrugged off pondering further on it as an unnecessary exercise and set to preparing the place for the night.

We checked for booby traps and mines as well as we could by moonlight, cleared an area by the one wall that still seemed to be mostly intact, and bedded down after a meal of cold C rations. Two by two we were to rotate sentry duty every two hours till dawn.

"Just in case the drug lord comes back," some wannabe comic quipped.

Upon overhearing that particular witticism, the sergeant thought it appropriate to regale us with a little bedtime story about a Japanese patrol he'd heard of that had neglected to post a sentry overnight. A small Ghurkha contingent, noted for their stealthy night manoeuvres, silently decapitated all but one of the sleeping soldiers. Before evaporating back into the surrounding jungle, they placed the severed heads in an inward facing circle around the single remaining and still sleeping Japanese soldier. Upon waking up in the morning and seeing what surrounded him, he promptly, and I think quite understandably, chose to commit hara-kiri.

The story was lent credibility by Wilful's assertion that he had known of the very same Ghurkhas that had carried out that particular operation in Burma in the spring of '42.

There were no further comments, witty or otherwise, about sentry duty, or anything else for that matter, only a silent and rather apprehensive though hasty retreat to waiting bedrolls.

The wind picked up considerably during the night and a few of the corrugated sheets rattled and clattered in straining protest. A positive aspect of the otherwise disquieting wind was that it helped shift away the remainder of the cloud cover revealing not only the moon but also a myriad of stars. Tonight we would sleep beneath a dome of brilliant white diamonds that seemed to reflect and amplify the pale glow of the moon. Some few of us lay, for a time, marvelling at a sight that the city boys among us rarely had an opportunity of seeing. Finally, however, we all drifted off.

Just as I awoke for my stint at sentry duty, there was a loud crack that sounded not unlike a rifle shot. Before I could realise what that sound signified, a large roof beam had collapsed onto where the Kid and I were bedded down. It wedged us tightly together so that we could not, and dare not, even try to extricate ourselves.

The wind, it seemed, had done a good deal more than merely shift a few clouds away. It had also helped bring down part of a previously weakened section of the structure as well.

Talk about being in the wrong place at the wrong time!

The Kid had taken the worst of the impact and seemed to be unconscious. The beam had struck him across the back of the head and shoulders and had somehow pushed him wedge like against me. A large cross member had crashed across my lower chest and pinned me securely to the wall. My head was all I could move, and then only marginally. I could hardly breathe, and the pain was intense.

The Kid moaned once and I could feel a warm liquid trickle course over my hand.

"Sarge, Sarge!" I managed to croak.

"Yes, yes, I'm here," he said. "You sure picked a *bonzer* bloody spot to bed down, didn't you, bucko?"

"We won't be able to move any of this shit till we can see what we're doing by daylight," said Wilful. "Just hang in there, okay?"

"I don't think I'll be going very far," I managed. "How does the Kid look?"

"Not too good," said the sergeant. "You just try and be still unless you want the rest of this shit hole to come down on top o' you."

Dawn never seemed to take so long to arrive as it did that day.

When there was finally enough light to see by, the sarge and two others tried to heft the roof beam off the Kid. That, however, only succeeded in levering the cross member even more painfully against me and setting the rest of our end of the structure to creaking ominously.

By mid morning, the rest of the group had managed to reinforce the wall against which we were pinned. Then, very gingerly, two of them hauled the beam off the Kid, while three others took the strain off the cross beam that pinned me so effectively to the spot.

The Kid, however, was far beyond caring. He was dead. His skull had been severely fractured as well as both shoulder blades and he must have bled out internally, according to our field medic.

Almost half an hour later they had freed me. Amazingly there were no broken bones, but I had one hell of a time breathing in more than short gasps. Although I had received multiple gashes and contusions, it didn't seem that a lung had been punctured, because, as our field medic, a PFC Silas (Corky) Corcoran, said, "He's not blowing red bubbles."

Wonderful, Dr. Bloody Smart Ass!

After a discussion about my condition, whether or not to leave me and one other as guard and just continue on themselves, the sergeant thought it more prudent for all of us to stay together and to bivouac there for another night. I said that I thought I would be able to make it after a bit of a rest. I had no way of actually knowing that, but I just felt that it was the thing to say. The sergeant and Wilful just exchanged glances and grinned.

While the group erected a shelter at the other end of the structure with old timber and corrugated sheets, I tried my legs out with the help of a Private Marsden. Although he didn't seem overly enthusiastic about playing nurse maid to me, the sarge gave him no option. He was even less pleased when he was later ordered to dig my personal "potty hole" when Nature called to me.

By evening, I was breathing a bit easier and could walk unaided for some distance, but my ribs were still excruciatingly painful. Fortunately, the field medic had a good supply of morphine, of which I took immediate advantage.

PFC Corky Corcoran, our field medic and Company leprechaun, said that he'd never seen anything quite like it. Apparently Corky hadn't seen enough of human strife and conflict in his war torn birthplace of Dublin, so he took his nursing skills to the American military.

Although my lower ribs were slightly pushed in, they didn't seem to be fractured. However, they still weren't reconforming to their natural position as they should have done by that time. He didn't think that binding them would be of any benefit.

"Sure and it's a bloody marvel t'me," he said in the sing song brogue that I'm sure he'd still have when he was ninety.

Just take a couple of aspirins and call me in the morning, I thought sardonically to myself. *Thanks a bunch, Corky.*

CHAPTER 17

Private Phillip "Pip" Marsden, my reluctant nurse maid and personal latrine digger, had taken his basic training at Fort Bragg—the one in North Carolina. When, in an effort at generating some kind of rapport with him, I had mentioned that I also trained at a Fort Bragg at about the same time, he said that he was surprised he hadn't seen me there. I told him it had been the one in northern California. He'd never heard of it, he told me with a certain amount of pomposity, indicating that if *he* hadn't heard of it then surely I must be mistaken.

He was, not to put too fine a point on it, a bit on the snooty side; he was of the refined Carolinian accent of a long-ruined, but still arrogant, Carolinian cotton plantation family.

After that exchange, I more or less curbed my efforts at developing a rapport.

He was a bit of a strange one in other respects as well. Aside from being a complete *neat-freak*, which I didn't necessarily think was a bad thing, he was also a consummate *clean-freak*. Now, I don't believe that there's anything particularly wrong with cleanliness, but his virtue was more of a vice.

He was accustomed, he had said, to bathing or showering two or three times a day. How he had managed that during basic training, however, I wasn't quite interested enough to inquire about, so I just put it down to a bit more of his pompous bullshit. He even had his own specially made soap, of which he had brought several bars with him.

This soap admittedly was very pleasant smelling, but as it contained pumice, I was amazed that he had any skin left after two or three applications a day. As it was, and not surprisingly, Pip Marsden hadn't a trace of body hair, except on the top of his head; no chest hair, no armpit hair and not even a whisper of pubic hair. Although I didn't care much to dwell on it, I couldn't help but feel that it was probably due to the pumice in his *designer* soap.

I could only very vaguely imagine his mental turmoil at not having sufficient water now for his two or three daily ablutions. There was, of course, rain water (and plenty of that just lately). This we caught, whenever we could, in our mess cans. However, that was hardly sufficient to his needs, because at least some of it had to be drunk.

Once, he thought that he would bathe by rolling naked in the ever wet marsh grass. This seemed to work quite acceptably until, to his discomfort and chagrin, he very soon discovered the land crabs that abounded there.

The adult crabs, apparently male and female alike, were each about the size of a large man's hand, quite aggressive and could move like lightening. They seemed like very bad tempered bastards and could also give you quite a nasty nip if you happened to linger for too long in their paths.

Exactly where he had been nipped during the first and last such exploit, he never volunteered any information on, and none of us were really curious enough to ask about. However, from then on, he simply, though inadequately, satisfied his ablutionary requirements with one of his monogrammed washcloths. It was quite the sight to see him standing naked and attempting to wash his six foot, five inch, hairless frame at the edge of the marsh.

It occurred to more than me that he would have made an excellent target for the enemy. Perhaps it even occurred to the sergeant, because he never put a halt to that particular bathing ritual.

It mystified me that Pip hadn't acquired a commission so he could've lived something of the lifestyle he so obviously craved. However, when I inquired about it early on in my attempts at rapport building, he quite menacingly told me to mind my own fucking business. I didn't ask a second time, though, partly due to his acerbic response, lack of personal funds, and family monetary embarrassment would have been my first guess.

So that was "Pip" Marsden. He despised that nickname, and I thought it quite inappropriate as well. He *should* have been nicknamed PITA (acronymic for Pain In The Ass).

Some years later I ran into Sergeant Gorman in a Seattle tavern. The revelation he imparted to me left me dumb struck, but it certainly answered some of the questions I'd pondered regarding Pip's hostile attitudes.

The old war horse and I had been doing some inevitable and liquor fuelled reminiscing, when out of the blue he said, "You knew, of course, that Pip was a homo, didn't you? I even think that he might have been game for the Kid's frame. That's probably why he didn't like you too much—you being so close to the Kid and all."

Then seeing my amazement, he continued: "Oh yah, a regular three dollar bill, Pip was. It tore his guts out because he didn't dare apply to West Point in case it all came out."

"He told you all that?" I asked. I was incredulous.

"Naw, naw. Not to begin with, anyway. One night on leave, I saw him comin' out of Sung's Pleasure Palace in Saigon arm in arm with some young gook guy. He saw me and dropped his *date* like a Black Widow, scuttled over, and offered to buy me a drink. We got pretty well oiled and then it all sorta' came tumblin' out o' him, about his family's rejection and about his dashed hopes for West Point. All of it. By the end of it all, he was blubbering like a kid, and I kinda felt sorry for him, faggot or not."

"But why in hell did he join up with the regulars then?" I asked.

"Who knows?" he said. "Maybe he just liked being around *real men* hoping it would rub off or somethin'. Maybe he just hated Commies enough. Who knows. Take your best guess."

As I say, it explained a lot. Homosexuality was actually illegal in some states at that time, and very likely was in one of the "good ole boy" states like South Carolina where Pip was from. The punishments were apparently quite severe, and time spent in a southern penitentiary for homosexuality wouldn't have been mistaken for being pleasant, to say the least. All his odd attitudes probably stemmed from a sense of shame, fear of discovery, and one frustration coming hard on the heels of another.

After hearing all of that, I couldn't help "kinda" feeling sorry for the arrogant bugger myself, "faggot or not."

CHAPTER 18

I am reasonably sure that virtually every school class, every office, and every blue collar work place has at least one: the clown, the jokester, the prankster. The military is apparently no exception. Owl Platoon's answer to the class clown was PFC Butko Zwyzic.

Now, I have to say that personal name recall has always been something of a challenge for me, but a name like Butko Zwyzic has a way of indelibly imprinting itself in one's memory. Perhaps not surprisingly, after his enlistment he was immediately tagged with the nickname, "Swizzle Stick."

The PFC sort of resembled a swizzle stick physically as well as by name. He was tall and very gangly—rangy, I guess would be the best descriptive term for his build, and I'm positive that he was born a comedian. It was often said that he probably peed in the eye of the delivery doctor that gave him his first ass smack.

During my partial convalescence in that humid Cambodian jungle, he would regale me with comical stories and anecdotes from his early years in Poland, to which his family had fled during some insurrection in his homeland of Yugoslavia. He was very quick-witted and could apparently find humour in just about any situation, and he frequently did.

Not infrequently was Pip the butt of a comical Swizzle Stick barb or two. Pip didn't like him much and made it fairly obvious. However, being the innate coward that he was, Pip would resort only to sneers and glares and nothing more.

Swizzle Stick would try and keep me from dwelling on my physical pain and sense of loss regarding the Kid by amusing me with those stories. However, I must confess that the tears in my eyes were as much from the pain that laughing caused as from the laughter itself. He meant well, though. He was like the brother I never had and it was with a sense of true brotherhood that we were reacquainted long afterwards at Fort Lewis in Washington state.

CHAPTER 19

There was certainly an intriguing, if not bewildering, cross section of humanity that I came across during my enlistment and tour of duty. Each of these men were quite different from the other, and each of them interesting in their own way. If nothing else, the contemplation of it all helped to cut down on the boredom of idle times between ops. After all, you could only play so many games of cards, or whatever, before that too became tedious and as bad as the boredom itself. Reading material was definitely at a premium, so aside from the inevitable T.V. repeats and listening to radio the only other thing to while away the time with was people watching, and the variety was all like some kind of sociologist's or psychologist's wet dream.

Then there was Walter "the Pigeon" Kravitz. The Pigeon nickname was mainly tagged to him because of his craving for sun flower seeds and not, apparently, just because of his skinny legs that turned bright pink with the slightest exposure to sunlight.

How he came to be in the army remains something of a mystery to this day. He was a nervous, bookish type with a physical structure that seemed as ill-suited to sporting a military uniform as a wire coat rack.

After some idle base camp time record probing, out of a mixture of shameless curiosity and the ever nagging boredom, it was determined that he hadn't in fact been drafted, as had been assumed. That bit of intelligence only deepened the mystery as to his presence in the army.

The Pigeon, although tight-lipped about most of his personal life, had expressed an avid interest in journalism. The military did have its own journalism branch, but one didn't necessarily have to steep oneself in the thick of a theatre of operations to perform its function successfully. It was unclear whether or not he had ever approached the military about pursuing his ambition. In any event he remained a regular "grunt" throughout his two hitch military career, and never attained a rank higher than PFC in the administration office pool. It seemed that his ambition for a military career died a protracted and languishing death after he voluntarily enlisted.

He did exercise his penchant for writing by starting a novel during the final week of boot camp, though. He said it helped to ease the tension generated by the prospect of going to Vietnam. I was left to wonder whether that tension was because of fear or excitement at the expectation. Again, he never elucidated. However, regardless of the cause, the tension must have been ongoing because by the time of his discharge in 1975, he had penned something in excess of twelve hundred pages in his cramped and tiny handwriting.

No one that I talked to about it had ever heard of it being published, or even what it was all about. Perhaps it was about nothing at all except tension relief.

On the topic of tension relief, the only time that I ever saw him truly come to life was when we went on leave to Saigon. There, he would go absolutely wild about the dizzying array of available hookers. He could go through a half dozen of them in the course of a seventy two hour leave. I'm not absolutely certain if he ever actually slept during a leave. I suppose he thought that he'd better make hay while the sun shone, because he very likely wouldn't have had much of an opportunity back home.

The Pigeon was truly a strange little fellow, but not really unlikeable. Aside from curious, I guess you could have called him merely inoffensive and unprepossessing.

CHAPTER 20

When I could once again sling my pack and rifle, we set off, skirting the edge of the marsh so that we could readily duck for cover if the need arose. Fortunately the rain had held off for a time. The downside was that the unremitting heat and humidity were virtually suffocating and made the ongoing slog almost unbearable—at least for me.

We had spent two nights in that decrepit shed, and always kept at least one ear peeled for any untoward creaks or groans from the structure. Those were two restless and bug infested nights that we could ill afford if we were to complete our mission and return to the river in time for evacuation. At least the land crabs didn't seem to want to bunk in with us. Perhaps they were smarter than we gave them credit for.

We would have bivouacked elsewhere, but there just wasn't anywhere else except the dense jungle or the too open and too boggy marsh.

Because of the heat and humidity, we had wrapped the body of Private Thomas "The Kid" Wakefield in his poncho and dug a temporary grave for him as soon as we could. With any luck, we or some other group would be able to retrieve his body later and return him to his family. I couldn't help but get a lump in my throat as we lowered him into that shallow hole. I'm sure the Kid never expected to end up like that: dead on a non-combat mission. *A walk in the park*, as the sergeant had said.

"Don't sweat it too bad. He was a good kid, but shit has a way of happenin'," said Wilful, always the bloody philosopher.

"Yes, Tom-tom was a good kid, though more than a little naïve," said Pip in his usually pompous fashion. However, even that statement coming from Pip seemed downright maudlin.

We were heading due north-west now, towards the last estimated coordinates that we had for the four missing marines. Barring any more "shit happenin'," we thought we'd be there in two more days, and back to the river again in four, maybe five, tops.

What was it that the Scottish bard once said about the best laid plans of mice and men?

The open marsh eventually came to an end and we were forced to machete our way through mostly moderate jungle. I say "we" only figuratively, because I wouldn't have been able to swing a machete had my life depended on it. That was yet one more reason for Pip to resent me, although no one else seemed to.

"Don't worry about it," said Wilful. "It'll take his mind of the lack of bathing water. Also, while he's

ragging your ass, he's leaving everyone else alone."
He chuckled heartily at his own wit.

Every cloud has a silver lining.

Probably according to Pip, it was all my fault that
our mission was dragging on. In all likelihood, he
would have been most concerned that his soap supply
wouldn't last.

Six days after starting out, after being stalled for two and
then getting ourselves lost for another two, we literally
stumbled across a small village inhabited by about
thirty men, women, and children. While they certainly
seemed surprised and initially a bit apprehensive at
seeing us appear out of the jungle, they were friendly
enough.

By this time we were a sorry looking sight to be sure.
Our food was running very low and our clothes were
literally starting to rot from our bodies and hung on us
in tatters. We had long since dispensed with our useless
underwear, which gave the vermin fewer places to hide.
We all suffered from an Asian form of pediculosis as
well as erysipelas, a nasty skin infection. Oh, we were
a grim looking sight, even to each other.

I can't begin to imagine what the natives must have
thought of our wretched appearance. Although they
weren't all that healthy looking themselves, we must
have looked like the ragged, starving country cousins
by comparison.

Out of dire necessity due to our current predicament, we deliberately chose to ignore the directive that we weren't supposed to initiate contact with the locals, and they gladly provided us with what food they could spare and whatever homemade remedies they could concoct for our ailments. Strictly speaking, I suppose we didn't really *initiate* contact as much as blunder into it anyway.

Wilful could speak with them, after a fashion, and found out that the four marines we were looking for had been taken away by what sounded like one of the Khmer Rouge rebel, splinter groups that the sergeant had heard of. The four hadn't been seen since and had to be presumed dead. However, the Khmer Rouge had returned several times.

It was beginning to look as though we wouldn't be finding our quarry any time soon—at least not within the allotted timeframe—and then probably not still alive in any case. More than a few of us shuddered to think of what their fates might have been. The Khmer Rouge weren't renowned for their humanitarian handling of prisoners.

The villagers used to raise pigs and a little wild rice, and that's what constituted the bulk of their diet along with some tubers they dug and whatever wild fruit they could find.

Then the rebel group started returning periodically to relieve them of whatever food they could carry away with them. They also took their pleasures with some of the more comely village women. In my opinion, there weren't very many of them, so I guessed that the ones thus used were *well* used.

Wilful had communicated to the villagers that an event special to our customs was coming up on the following day: namely Christmas. This, they said, they had heard of, although they were of no recognisable religious affiliation. To their credit and unexpected generosity, they insisted we stay another day, and that they would provide a celebration for us. In our debilitated state and realising that ours would most likely be a failed mission in any case, the sergeant gratefully accepted on our behalf.

Not many modern day Christians, I think, would have been quite as hospitable or generous in the circumstances.

I spent my first Christmas, away from the company of relatives, in this little clutch of huts. It all seemed most un-Christmas like; a hot and almost unbearably humid setting that was not in the slightest reminiscent of a typical Christmas card scene.

For Christmas dinner, there was cured pork, wild rice steeped and steamed in some kind of homemade liquor, and something that resembled yams. Afterwards, and somewhat incongruously, we sang Christmas carols around a communal camp fire while the villagers laughed and clapped. The poor buggers had little enough else to be joyous about.

CHAPTER 21

I had spent the previous Christmas amongst family, neighbours, and old friends at my parent's place. It had been the usual festive affair with laughter, stories about previous Christmases, and how they weren't the same as they used to be, how it was all getting over commercialised and so on. There were the usual noisy, hyperactive children, whom, I've always thought, Christmas is really mostly for. There was eating and drinking (usually to excess) and an exhibition of camaraderie and joie de vivre that was seldom exhibited at any other time of the year, but, at least in retrospect, it was and is all a great and, I think, a much needed diversion from the everyday affairs of most of us.

But oh, when it snowed, which it rarely does on the southwest coast of Canada, it was all an added bonus that people would venture out into whether it was bare-handed in slippers and dressing robes, or be-mittened with parkas and snow boots. The magic of the season seemed to be magnified by the event of a little crystallised moisture falling on the occasion.

The day had started, as it always did, with a flurry of last minute baking, turkey stuffing, basting and roasting, house cleaning (though that had only been done the day before), table setting, and last minute decorating. The heated discussions and arguments about the previous round of frenetic house decorating, inside and out, had been momentarily forgotten in the heat of completing a task that, in reality, was usually overdone in any case. Ah, but the final result was well worth the harassment that the preparations had included.

For some time, my father had been badgering me to get married and start producing grandchildren. He thought that I was awfully "slow" about getting involved with women. I told him I wasn't about to leap precipitously into marriage just to satisfy his yen for grandparenthood. I didn't point out that he hadn't performed a particularly exemplary job as a parent so what would make him think he might do better as a *grand*parent—it was the season to be jolly, after all. But, undeterred, he continued on the lookout for suitable *breeding stock* for me.

One of the neighbours had a pretty, young daughter that old Dad thought would be eminently suited to the role (according to him, she had good, childbearing hips), and as chance would have it, the poor unsuspecting girl was at my parent's house for the festivities.

All through the evening, Dad surreptitiously (he thought) arranged for us to be seated together in the living room, at the supper table, and later in the family room for after dinner drinks, et cetera. Then, throughout the evening he would make random comments about how well we looked together; how we seemed so well suited for each other; and how did we like kids and the like.

In this tack, he had enlisted the willing aid of the more than enthusiastic girl's father who seemed only too well disposed to concur in all pronouncements, as well as adding some of his own odd notions to the mix.

Subtlety was hardly Dad's strong suit at the best of times, but those proceedings went way beyond the pale in tactlessness, even given that all was well and truly fuelled by an overabundance of liquor.

Eventually, to stem the embarrassment for both of us, I asked the girl if I could walk her home. Dad probably thought, *Ah, at last! This is it!* The poor girl just about fell over herself accepting my offer to get away from the place, and that probably tended only to verify my dad's thoughts about a future *union* with a hopefully fecund baby machine.

After walking her home, apologising for my dad's thoughtless and embarrassing behaviour and then walking around the neighbourhood to cool off a bit, I arrived back to find our respective fathers passed out together on the settee in the living room. I could only imagine what their conversation entailed before they had finally dropped off with those self-satisfied expressions still present on their flushed faces.

The neighbour girl did get married in my absence—although I'm certain that my absence had nothing to do with it—to a fellow she had been going with off and on and for some time. Perhaps the Christmas incident had been the final catalyst in making the decision on her eventual course. Given the tenor of the event, it's not entirely beyond the realms of possibility.

When she was seen to be dating the man who would eventually become her husband, my dad just thought that I'd *lost out* yet again because of my dilatory ways.

"My God but you're slower 'n' molasses in January, *boy*! Y'ain't queer or somethin', are ya? 'Cause if you're thinking of joining up, you'll find that they take a dim view of that sort of thing in the army, y'know."

Oh, very charming!

So that was my last Christmas at home before I had decided that I should apply myself to what I thought was a more worthwhile pursuit. It was a memorable Christmas in more ways than one, but I must say that I certainly missed it in the current situation and regardless of the negative aspects. Perspective is everything, after all.

CHAPTER 22

Whether it was due to a surfeit of homemade liquor, or gaiety, or mind-numbing weariness, or a combination of all three, we had neglected to post sentries through the night. That proved unwise, because as we emerged from our hut, we were met by a half dozen men in ragged clothes that made ours look like Sunday-go-to-meeting apparel. However, unlike us, they were armed to the teeth.

With four Kalashnikovs and, incongruously, two M16's aimed at us and barked orders, which, though dimly understood, were clear enough in their meaning, we had little choice except to comply and trot out to the central clearing. I'm sure most of us wondered if that was going to be our last Christmas.

We were made to squat in an inward facing circle on the ground, with our hands clasped to the backs of our heads, while they rummaged around through our kits, and brutally harassed the villagers.

Fortunately, we had had the foresight to cache our rifles in the jungle before we came into the village. So after searching us, all they came away with were our side arms. They then locked us in an abandoned pig shed while they decided our fate.

We spent the better part of a sweltering week in the stifling stench of that windowless shed. During that time, the skies opened up and the rains began again with a renewed though not refreshing vigour. That seemed to knock the already teetering sanity of Pip Marsden right off its base. He ranted incessantly about needing a bath, the loss of his precious soap and silver handled toothbrush, and where the hell were his monogrammed towels. He'd pound and butt his head on the walls until his fists and forehead were raw, and rave at our captors through chinks in the door.

No amount of reasoning had the slightest modicum of success. We tried to quieten him with no apparent effect. He seemed beyond any lucid comprehension. We tried to subdue him physically, but he fought back with the strength of a mad man, and in that confined space and with our depleted physical strength, there was little we could do that didn't seem to incite him to further rage.

In one such set to, I was kicked in my already screaming ribs. I thought and felt as though that was going to be *curtains* for me. I remained unconscious in the stinking muck on the floor for about an hour.

Finally, at the end of the second day, the rebels' tenuous patience gave out completely. They gun butted Pip into submission, dragged him from the shed, stripped him bare of his tattered uniform, and tied him to a post in the centre of the village. Being naked for all to see was apparently the ultimate humiliation for these people and the rebels apparently thought it was absolutely hilarious.

"Well, at least he'll be getting his bloody bath," quipped Wilful as we watched the rain lashing down on the naked, squirming and shrieking Pip.

For nearly two more days, he raved practically without let up in the almost ceaseless downpour; then, finally and mercifully, passed out. He was certainly tough, if not very lucid. The rebels, by now tired of the diversion, cut him loose and threw him back in with the rest of us. Then they did a surprising thing: they merely took our medical supplies, side arms, and ammunition and left. I guess they must have thought that we were of no threat to them in our present condition, and that it would satisfy them more if we died a more miserable and lingering death in the jungle. Perhaps they thought that we were deserters; who knows.

By this time, without food and only the water that trickled through the leaking roof, most of us could hardly stand and had contracted dysentery as well. However, it was worse for poor Pip. He had contracted pneumonia, or some other pernicious lung infection. He only lasted into the third night in his raving delirium and continuous and agonising bouts of coughing up great gobs of blood. Then we buried him just outside the village at the edge of the jungle.

Pip was certainly a pompous prig, but he didn't deserve that kind of an end.

After ten days in that jungle village, another dead body and a failed mission, we decided that, able or not, we needed to get the hell out of there before the rebels decided to return. Those wonderful villagers supplied us with what food they could spare, and seemed genuinely sorry to see us go.

We retrieved our rifles and, minus our packs, which the rebels had commandeered, we set out as quickly as our quivering legs would allow. Needless to say, we didn't break any land speed records.

Each time I had to stop to relieve myself from either end, and not infrequently from both ends simultaneously, the pain from my injured ribs just about made me pass out. Although Wilful was exhibiting symptoms of the malaria that he had picked up years before in Burma, he seriously thought that I was going to be the next one that they would have to "pull the sod over."

All I can very dimly recall of that mind numbing return trek was passing the spot where I had stepped into that dead body. The body was no longer in evidence, (the land crabs had probably had a feast) but that image and the penetrating stench would stay vividly with me, accompanied by silent shudders, for many years to come. The single event of that return trek that I can clearly recall is arriving at our original bivouac site to find a squad of U.S. Marines just about to set out in search of us.

We had taken eight days to complete that virtually non-stop return slog, and miraculously without any further casualties.

The first thing that struck me was the irony of it all. We had been sent in to retrieve lost Marines, and here *they* were to retrieve *us*. The war must surely be winding down if they could afford to send the much vaunted Marines after a squad of overdue *grunts*.

It didn't really matter. If I'd had the energy and could have stood up straight, I would have kissed each and every one of them. As it was, instead of kissing them, I finally gave in to the pain and misery and passed out into a waiting Marine's arms.

I remember thinking, much later, how unfortunate it is that one can't be aware of the bliss of that sweet, engulfing blackness. But then, I suppose, it would defeat the whole purpose of the event.

It would be more than three decades until anyone from the Khmer Rouge leadership would be brought to trial, if not complete and exacting justice, for the atrocities that they perpetrated on anyone unfortunate enough to fall into their clutches. The atrocities, though indistinguishable from war crimes, could not apparently be referred to as "war crimes" since "war" had never officially been declared.

CHAPTER 23

I spent six weeks recuperating in the military wing of an Hawaiian hospital; the last two weeks of which were as an outpatient.

I slowly regained some of the weight that I'd lost. The bleeding, weeping cankers that had covered most of my body finally healed leaving reddish depressions in my skin. These would take a few years to be reduced to merely slightly darker patches of skin; some of which I still have to this day. The ribs would finally reconform to something approximating their original placement. However, even many years later, I still don't have what could be described as a symmetrical rib cage.

The unorthodox displacement of the ribs, without them actually having been fractured or otherwise dislocated, was a source of wonderment to the many doctors and specialists that came to view, prod, and poke them.

One of my hospital mates, Nathan "Nate" Duchene (he of the pock marked, hawk's face), had offered to get me some extra drugs for the pain—or *recreation*—or whatever. Apparently he had also served in that capacity in 'Nam and had some willing contacts on the islands.

I had become aware early on that drug dealing had been a widespread enterprise in 'Nam for a lot of the GIs, but, until becoming acquainted with Nate, I had no idea of the magnitude of that enterprise.

In Tan Son Nhut, Nate had also run quite a successful prostitution ring. He'd had between twelve and fifteen girls, and even a few young boys, working for him at any one time. His income had been so lucrative that, at the end of his first tour, he had volunteered for a second and then a third.

When I asked him if he hadn't been concerned about getting shipped into combat, he merely bared those big, yellowed teeth in an approximation of a grin, winked at me, and said that it always paid to have friends in high places. When pressed to elaborate, he indicated there had been no less than a full colonel on the "take" to more than just him.

Then he had made a near fatal error. There had been a fairly large shipment of everything from marijuana to cocaine to heroin that he hadn't trusted anyone but himself to pick up and deliver. Unfortunately, both the pickup and the drop were to be made very close to the DMZ, in Phan Rang, on the east coast north of Saigon.

Nate thought this was a great bit of luck because he wouldn't have to store it or even keep it long before he got his pay-off. Unfortunately, the Viet Cong decided on an offensive, launched from the South China Sea, on the very night and in the very vicinity of the delivery.

He had to watch helplessly as the boat that had brought his booty was blown sky high, along with his dreams of a high life Stateside. Then he was caught in a cross fire between the Viet Cong and Marines.

When the Marines found him the next morning, he was in pretty bad shape, but lucky to have escaped with his life. He had received multiple hits of shrapnel and a couple of minor bullet wounds. However, the worst wound for him, he had said, was the loss of a life on *easy street.*

His career was at an end because he would receive a compulsory medical discharge after that debacle and the possible repercussions to his high ranking military benefactor. Embarrassing questions might be asked about why Nate had been in that particular area with an unauthorised truck and a driver.

The absolute irony was that he had pulled all those strings to get a relatively safe assignment in Saigon and then had blown it all in one great, stupid attempt to make the one really big score.

Another irony, of somewhat lesser import, was that he spent more time recuperating from the *clap* (gonorrhoea) from too much sampling of his own *girly wares* than he did from gunshot and shrapnel wounds. It was certainly fortunate for him that it was before the era of HIV and AIDS.

However, he didn't stay down for long. The last I heard of his ongoing escapades was a second or third hand story of him running drugs and girls in San Francisco. He had evidently learned his craft well because the way he was apparently living wasn't, it seemed, too far shy of *the high life on easy street* that he had dreamed of.

Unfortunately for Nathan Duchene, a couple of years later he succumbed to a hail of bullets from some competitor who had apparently taken extreme umbrage at his vaunting success.

CHAPTER 24

Way before Burt Gorman had become Master Sergeant Gorman, he had been supremely pissed off that he had joined the Aussie Army too late to be called into active overseas duty during World War II. He'd really wanted to kick some Jap ass, he had said, but had been relegated to Home Security partly because of his youth and partly because of the threat of a Japanese invasion.

That probably had more to do with the fact that he had been only sixteen when he joined up. While the military certainly might not have known that for sure, they must have suspected. He was big for his age and had the bluster of an older man, but there were other things that pointed to his youth in spite of all that. However, Australia was hard pressed for military manpower at that particular time and so they made do with what they could get, basically.

His father, uncle, and an older brother had all joined up at the outset, and had all distinguished themselves in various campaigns. That was motivating factor enough for young Burt. However, his uncle and brother being captured and sent to a Japanese POW camp was the deciding factor in acquiring a phony birth certificate and joining up himself.

Young Burt simply refused to be content with waiting for the "Japs" to come to him to be able to kick some ass. Then, after months of badgering the brass for a transfer to an actual fighting unit, they had finally apparently had enough of it and shipped him off to join his father's regiment with ANZAC for the deciding assault on Okinawa. The brass may even have thought that the tactic would have put a permanent end to the thorn in their sides because that endeavour was expected to be a brutal one.

Only a week into it, he watched his father die with a bullet through the throat.

Then, after the Japanese surrender, he and his mother were summoned to the docks of Sidney harbour to collect the remains of his brother and uncle. Their bodies had been so grossly maltreated and emaciated that their coffins had to remain sealed and buried as they were.

Anyone else might have said, "Enough is enough," but Burt Gorman's resolve was set and immutable. He continued serving with ANZAC until the Vietnam conflict erupted in 1961, by which time he had become a much decorated sergeant. Then, somehow he managed to wangle a transfer to an American regiment where he was not only welcomed with open arms but promoted to the rank of Staff Sergeant.

Say what you will about the American military, but they certainly knew how to pick an NCO.

However, I'll never forget the apoplectic, ranting tirade he went into when, many years later, it was announced that the United States Vice President would attend the funeral to honour the dead Japanese emperor, Hiro Hito.

While on a quest for some thirst slaking, I had run into the sergeant in a Seattle tavern on a hot, sunny Saturday afternoon. He had apparently had a head start on me; he had been holding forth for some liquor fuelled length of time with his usual verbal vitriol on the subject.

"Imagine the absolute brass balls of that simpering, gutless administration wanting to honour that inhuman, black hearted, lunatic, Nip bastard that was the cause of so much bloody suffering. The scum-sucking, ass kissing bastards! Let by-gones be by-gones, bullshit! That pompous little shit-lick was a bloody war criminal in anyone's book."

Oh, Burt Gorman was something less than thrilled at that particular U.S. gesture.

CHAPTER 25

Before I was even able to shuffle around the hospital ward with the aid of a walking frame, I was trundled in a wheelchair down to the hospital basement for a debriefing. I'm not sure if it was a fitting venue or not, but the proceedings took place in a room next to the hospital morgue. Perhaps it was because it was isolated and relatively secure. Perhaps they thought they should strike while the iron was hot in the event I died before they had their chance; in which possibility I would have been suitably situated. In any case, it was certainly secure, nice and cool and very quiet—surreally quiet.

Had I not been in so much discomfort, I might have been quite impressed at the entourage of brass and their minions that gathered for the event. The best I could muster was mild surprise. There were no fewer than two captains, a major, who seemed to be the chairman of the event, a lieutenant from army intelligence, and *two* stenographers, not to mention two MPs at the door. I couldn't really be sure if the MPs were there to keep others out or to keep me from making a dash for it. That thought almost cracked me up and my grin received more than just a passing quizzical look.

"Do you find something amusing, Corporal?" snapped one of the captains, probably not particularly pleased to be there.

"Oh, no sir," I lied. "I just had a stitch, sir."

It occurred to me at the time that it all might have been slightly *over the top*. Then again, perhaps there wasn't all that much for them to do at that stage of the conflict, and what brass there was left in the area at least had to be seen to be busy.

There wasn't really all that much that I could clearly recount of our S and R mission, but officiousness seems second nature to the military and like I said, they had to be seen to be busy whether it was a fruitful effort or not.

They asked questions that even they must have realised I wouldn't have been capable of answering. I suppose that because of my NCO status, they felt somehow obligated to ask them anyway. I thought that it was a little more than surprising there wasn't a great deal of time spent on the fact we had countermanded the non-fraternisation edict. As a matter of fact, they actually seemed to appreciate the reasoning for it. Very understanding of them!

The whole exercise took slightly over two hours, during which time I wasn't even allowed to leave the room to relieve myself. With all the fluids the nurses had been pumping into me and my bladder catheter having been removed, it was something of a challenge, I can tell you, but security had to be maintained, didn't it?

I heard nothing more for three or four days, then the AI lieutenant brought the debriefing transcript for me to read over and sign. When I jokingly said I was surprised he had come personally instead of one of his minions, he grinned broadly and said he was flying back to Stateside in half an hour and needed the papers right away. The utter relief literally beamed from him like sunshine. Lucky dog! Now that he was leaving, he didn't seem such a bad sort after all.

Although I didn't realise it at the time, it would be quite some while until I could follow him back to the mainland.

That debriefing business certainly seemed like an odd hit and miss sort of thing to me. After my first mission at the DMZ, there was no debriefing of anyone except the platoon commander. Even with the advent of that very obviously sloppy security protocol, no one else was *interviewed*. Maybe they were just too damned embarrassed about the whole affair to want to delve too deeply into it all. As nobody knows how to cover their butts better than top military brass, maybe someone higher up than a mere platoon commander was culpable. Who knows? It all just appeared more than a little strange. Ah well, the military way, eh. Who else is capable of successfully plumbing those murky depths?

CHAPTER 26

When I was finally deemed fit enough to travel, I was flown back to the mainland, via Clark Air Base in the Philippines, and was shuttled up to Fort Lewis, Washington. There, I spent the final few months of my radically foreshortened enlistment shuffling papers and partying on the odd leave that I got, while I waited for my medical discharge papers to come through.

One day, about a week after I had arrived and while I was delivering some files to HQ, I ran into PFC Butko Zwyzic. He had been sent to Fort Lewis for the last few weeks of his hitch. That evening we got leave to go off base to reminisce and get hammered. Getting hammered for me was, at that time, an inexpensive affair because I was still recuperating on meds and still fairly underweight. However, we had a great time and had to do more than a little butt kissing when we arrived back to base hours late.

We traded addresses and promised to write often and send Christmas cards and such. He had been a good buddy to me when I needed one the most, and I fully intended to follow through with communications and perhaps the odd visit.

He was still the same old "Swizzle Stick"; he was full of good humour and comical anecdotes, as though he had just returned from holidays. More power to him. He would have little enough time left to enjoy himself.

Three weeks after his discharge and on his way home to a wife and two kids, Private First Class Butko Zwyzic was killed in a head-on crash with some lunatic piss-tank who had somehow crossed over to the wrong side of the I-5 highway.

Unfortunately, I didn't become aware of it until about a week after the funeral. I had been in hospital again with something of a relapse, otherwise I wouldn't have missed bidding a final farewell to my old bud for the world.

After my discharge papers finally came through, aided I'm sure by the event of my last relapse, I paid a visit to his widow, Marta, on my way back to Vancouver. To my astonishment, she said that Butko had told her all about me and what a great guy I was. He had called me a real *rock*.

Marta must have been a little taken aback at the sight of the emaciated "rock" that she answered the door to, but you would never have guessed it by the warm greeting I received. She tearfully welcomed me with open arms like a long lost brother.

For many years after, Marta and I corresponded, visited back and forth, and exchanged Christmas and birthday cards, little gifts, et cetera. I was even made honorary uncle to the two Zwyzic children. They were truly great kids, and they all felt like extended family.

Someone once asked me why I didn't just marry the woman and be done with it. Although she was a few years older than I and I'm sure that she would have made a wonderful wife, but I just couldn't screw her life up like that. I was still too screwed up myself without getting that closely involved with a woman and her two kids. Although I probably did love her (who wouldn't have?), I still had the presence of mind to recognise it just wouldn't be fair to anyone. Marta was far better off with the memory of a dead husband like Butko than a life with a live one like I was at the time.

Then, she too passed away from stomach cancer at the age of fifty-two. This lovely, caring, and gentle woman certainly didn't deserve that kind of an end, but then, neither did her husband deserve his ignominious end.

Her funeral brought back so many painful memories for me that, for a brief moment, I was almost sorry I went. However, those memories were more than made up for by reliving in my mind the many great memories we had all made together. Regardless, I owed at least that much to the memory of my old buddy, "Swizzle Stick," and in some small way, I felt that it made up for missing *his* funeral.

Even so many years later, I still keep in touch with the kids, who now have kids of their own.

The wheel of life just keeps turning.

CHAPTER 27

I've pondered the notion and definition of heroism for some considerable time. Ever since a teetering, slurring drunk accosted me in a bar and after someone else snidely and somewhat bitingly referred to me as a "war hero," I've thought about it. After a heroic attempt at focussing his bloodshot and watery eyes on me, the drunk asked me in an extremely wet-lipped fashion what the hell I thought a hero was, anyway.

Notwithstanding his state of advanced inebriation, I thought it was a worthwhile question. Unfortunately, I couldn't answer it, so, as I wiped his spittle spray from my shirt, I pondered. The drunk, meanwhile and presumably on his way to the toilets, staggered unerringly and head first into a post immediately rendering himself unconscious, at which point any answer that I may have given him would have done him very little good.

In my Oxford English Dictionary, a hero is defined in part as "a person who is admired for their courage or outstanding achievements." That definition may bring to mind all sorts of romanticised uncommon gallantry peculiar perhaps to our nostalgic inner view of knights on white chargers or dragon slayers. I suppose in an effort to clarify or qualify, another part of the definition reads: "(in mythology and folklore) a person of superhuman qualities."

I think it is too often suggested that heroes can be created by involvement in war or some other traumatic human event, and this occasionally somehow happens with the seemingly least likely of candidates. With those least likely candidates in mind, I believe courage is oftentimes displayed by a very ordinary person performing the simple act of plodding through life battling the day to day frustrations of common human interactions without taking the gas pipe or some other expedient ticket out of a fray commonly, if not blithely, referred to as *life*.

Unless one knows every infinitesimal part of a person's character, which I think would be a virtual impossibility, how could one be certain of knowing, without a shadow of doubt, whether or not that person would be capable of becoming a hero in the sense suggested by the Oxford English Dictionary's definition, or the romanticised interpretation of it?

It is also a predominant belief that only the good can be heroes. That seems to fly in the face of the fact that no definition of a hero remotely suggests that his heroic deeds need be for the common good. It also flies in the face of the fact that many have secretly, and often even openly, admired some form of criminal activity along with the criminal involved and viewed that criminal in heroic terms. Jesse James and Billy the Kid spring immediately to mind.

Heroism must therefore be a subjective concept. Although I didn't particularly like Nate Duchene or was even very comfortable in his company, I felt he was a hero in his own right. He had some very definite goals and dreams, and stalwartly overcame some considerable obstacles and adversities to realise them before his end came. Even Pip Marsden, whom I didn't like at all, could be considered a hero of sorts. He fought a devastating inner conflict for most of his life—certainly for all of his adult life, as abbreviated as it was.

In my estimation, certainly a more acceptable candidate for hero status would be Burt Gorman, because to a far greater degree he fulfilled the more common view of what a hero should be. But whether or not the sergeant could generally be considered an actual hero by anyone else, I considered him as such as well as a good and honourable friend.

Ditto for Swizzle Stick.

I suppose the question could be asked: do heroes really exist, or are they only people who do what they have to when pressed hard enough to do anything at all, regardless of good motives or selfish ones?

In the final analysis, I believe that displays of what may commonly be perceived as heroism are prompted primarily by our innate sense of self-preservation, which may or may not include the preservation of our own kind.

Hell, I may be a hero after all! Now, where the devil did that drunk get to?

CHAPTER 28

I have put off recording this for so many years because I really needed to get my head around the entire thing, and be able to talk or write about it when I could do so with relative ease and without regenerating the dreams that had been part of my life for so long. Coming to terms with it all took me down a long and arduous route, and many times I almost gave up to take the easier path of booze and drugs like so many of my more unfortunate contemporaries had done.

It was only about five years ago that I could sleep an entire night without experiencing some nocturnal visions of that painful, twisted part of my past.

After only a total of about three months in Southeast Asia, I had returned covered in weeping jungle-rot cankers, dangerously dehydrated, hardly able to walk (certainly not upright), with a pernicious lung infection and galloping dysentery, and almost forty pounds lighter. Apparently, I had been only days away from death, and I had been with a *non-combat* group. However, some others had not been quite as fortunate.

When I say *not quite as fortunate,* I don't refer, necessarily, to dying. Death, at least in my view, could be seen as being preferable to some of the alternatives that I have repeatedly witnessed.

It took almost six months to receive my medical discharge and DD-214 (discharge papers and record of service). In the meantime, after I had been released from the Hawaiian military hospital and flown back to the mainland, I was put on what was euphemistically referred to as *light duties* at Fort Lewis in Washington state. I guess the military just wanted to make absolutely certain I couldn't be of any further use to them *in the field*. They must have grudged the time and money they had expended in training and keeping me and then having to release me eight months shy of a full tour of duty.

I had, in fact, the dubious distinction of surviving the shortest military career on record at that time.

Surprisingly, by that time, I had been made a *full* corporal with the appropriate pay rate, which was approximately another twenty dollars or so a month. I always suspected that that and the Meritorious Service Medal I received had the ear marks of Master Sergeant Burt Gorman's influence. It certainly was my impression, at least, that there hadn't been much that one could have described as being particularly "meritorious" about my service to the military.

Aside from the physical injuries, I don't know for certain if I ever suffered from the newly recognised Post-Traumatic Stress Disorder (though there seemed to be every indication that I did) because the army never saw fit to refer any of us for psychiatric assessment or counselling. Hell, after we were discharged, they didn't particularly want to know *anything* about us; especially the *foreign* contingent.

We and the abysmally failed "conflict" were all a huge embarrassment to the mightiest military power on earth, and they seemed bound and determined to do everything in their power to put it all behind them, and to that end, the general public of the time were eagerly complicit. The sooner forgotten by all, the better.

It's only been very recently that the American government has given any meaningful acknowledgement to their Vietnam veterans and belatedly address themselves to an attempted healing regimen. Better late than never, I guess.

Although I had been awarded the customary Vietnam Service Medal as well as the Meritorious Service Medal, I didn't need or want any special recognition or sympathy; but for so many years I, and so many others worse off than I, needed some extended help that rarely, if ever, materialised. I don't know about the others, but all I felt comfortable with was just bottling it all up. I didn't talk to any of my old buddies about it. Hell, I haven't even seen more than one or two of them since the end of the "conflict." For many years, I didn't talk to *anyone* about it.

Then, about five years ago, when the dreams had seemed to become more tolerable and a lot less frequent, I had ventured to talk to a total stranger in a bar about it all. He had been a World War II veteran and he also reminded me quite a bit of my old platoon sergeant: tough but kindly, old Burt Gorman. That as well as being a stranger made talking about it all somehow more comfortable and a lot less intimidating. I felt that anyone who had never been embroiled in at least similar circumstances could not only *not* empathise but, in my experience, take a hostile attitude to it all as well as to the person involved.

The old vet and I struck an immediate sense of camaraderie with one another. We commiserated with each other about our separate experiences and talked generally and at some length about our perceptions of war and its aftermath. After about an hour or so, we merely drained our glasses and went our separate ways, each lost in our own thoughts.

That night I was, yet again, hunkered down in a spotting tower waiting for one of the exploding shells dropping around me to hit it, or a stray bullet to find its way into my enclosure. I was again sailing up the Mekong River under heavy enemy fire from the surrounding jungle. I was again stepping into and smelling that decomposing body in a moonlit Cambodian marsh (don't ever let anyone tell you that you can't experience the impression of scent in a dream). I was again trying to scrape the reeking gore off my boots. I was again being closeted in a stinking pig shed by the Khmer Rouge and awaiting a possibly very nasty and protracted death. I was again feverishly trudging many humid and sweltering miles hunkered over in excruciating agony like a dog humping a football. It played over and over in my mind like a film in a loop.

That was it! Even *then,* so many years later, the psychological wounds were still too fresh. I doubted then that it would ever end. Sometimes I even doubted my very sanity.

And what then of those who suffered greater torments than mine? What of those who would have to spend the rest of their lives not only emotionally wounded, but also physically crippled?

Now, so many years later, I have taken my time in writing this, just a little every three or four days. I just wanted to be certain that I wouldn't get bogged into that mental film loop again.

It's been three weeks, now, and so far only one fleeting dream. No more waking up tangled in the sheets and bathed in sweat. No more starting up in the night hearing the dying reverberations of my last scream. I seem to have *broken through*. I hope I have.

Some of my old sense of humour has even begun to return, although now it seems to be a little more on the darker side than it used to be. However, that may have as much to do with the almost inevitable cynicism that comes with aging as with my experiences in Southeast Asia. Whatever it is, it is also an improvement over the way I was for so many years.

At least I did come away from the whole episode having learned some valuable lessons. Probably one of the most valuable of those is that you must never become so afraid of dying that you ever lose sight of living. I think that sentiment is evinced in a modern song written and sung by people who I'm sure can have little notion of what it's all about.

Now in my late fifties, I've finally started a serious relationship. She's a lovely, loving, and patient woman who's had her own demons to conquer over the years; so she's also understanding. She seems to have conquered those demons both stoically and very successfully, so she realises what a protracted but worthwhile battle it can be.

Mom thinks that she's just the most wonderful person there could possibly be, so that's the best endorsement to me. Perhaps if Dad was still alive, he would have liked her as well, although it would have been far too late for us to supply him with the much desired grandkids.

I've also enrolled in some evening college courses and started dabbling in oil painting. I'm certainly no Rembrandt, but I find that putting some of my memories onto canvas affords me with a very satisfying release. Perhaps surprisingly, a lot of those painted images are not the gruesome depictions that you might think. A lot are of the gentle, affable villagers who were so incredibly kind to the bedraggled foreign soldiers who stumbled, half-starved, out of the jungle; they were so kind in the face of such dire consequences.

The courses help me better understand what has happened to me and at least some of my army buddies. They have also helped me to understand and temper my anger and frustration at the insanity of human conflict. Lastly, they have helped me to write this in a more comprehensible if not comprehensive fashion.

This story may not be Pulitzer Prize material, but I am amply satisfied that it has helped me along the road of healing. That is gratification enough.

I think that I may finally have arrived. I *hope* that I've finally arrived. It's been so long. It's been *too* long (and yet not long enough) since my ill-conceived enlistment and that flight into Vietnam; the flight into emotional mayhem: my flight into folly.

> *The most exquisite Folly is made of*
> *Wisdom spun too fine.*
>
> —Benjamin Franklin

*Military force—especially when wielded
by an outside power—cannot bring order
in a country that cannot govern itself.*

—Robert McNamara
US Secretary of Defence 1961-1968

AUTHOR'S POST SCRIPT

In closing, I'd just like to include a little factual anecdote that I picked up along the way. This won't intrinsically have anything whatsoever to do with the story that you have just read, but I thought that it was so interesting that I just had to share it with you, Dear Reader—that and the conclusion that I drew from it.

Also, this is my *forum* after all.

Anyway, apparently the landmark book, "Naked Came the Stranger," touted on the New York Best Sellers list in 1969, was actually a gag perpetrated to tweak the noses of the writer's nemeses: editors and publishers alike. It was cobbled together over a weekend by a group of twenty-five writers, who, probably while fuelled by various intoxicants, each worked on a different chapter. The book was credited to a Penelope Ashe, supposedly a Long Island housewife. As well as receiving glowing accolades from diverse critical pundits (those that REALLY know a story and its literary worth), "Naked Came the Stranger" sold almost a hundred thousand hardcover copies and about two million paperbacks in the first year.

The conclusion, not to mention the point to this most unorthodox departure from the "norm," is that in the face of the foregoing, it is my determined view this book may well have a chance of attracting the same glowing accolades from *on high*, not to mention the concomitant soaring sales from book stores, and equally concomitant royalties from the publisher (I blush uncontrollably even to mention the latter). My only hopes in that regard are that it realises all of that on its own more genuine merits and that I haven't also tweaked the noses of editors and publishers too sharply by exhibiting the unabashed temerity of including this post script.

At the risk of being accused of wantonly embracing over-loquaciousness, I feel compelled to include one last comment. In the course of any life, whether long, short, or otherwise, there exists the possibility of good fortune and of bad in more or less unequal portions. In your life, Dear Reader, my fervent wish is that there may be an abundance of the first accompanied by an utter absence of the second.

Jon Christensen

THE VERY END

Really!

ABOUT THE AUTHOR

Jon Christensen is a published lyric poet, the published author of magazine articles and essays, both anecdotal and philosophical, individual short stories and a book of short stories entitled *Flights of Fancy* for which his artistic inclination dictated that he design and develop his own cover.

He began short story writing at a relatively early age (about 14), but only for his own amusement and that of a few select friends. It never occurred to him to attempt publishing anything until many years later when his wife read some of his material, after which, as he puts it: *unrest was born.*

Raised as an only child in a small farming community in central Manitoba, Jon lived a rather isolated existence during his formative years. Consequently he became an introverted child, and as a result became an avid reader of just about anything he could lay his hands on. Eventually, he narrowed his field of particular interest down to mysteries, fantasies and the occult.

Quite early on, Edgar Allan Poe became an enduring favourite and was followed by Guy De Maupassant, H. G. Wells, Ray Bradbury and Jules Verne, to name just a few. Later, Stephen King, Dean Koontz and the

British authors, Ian Rankin and Peter Lovesey further stimulated his imagination.

Historical novels also captivated him and were the catalyst for his love of the intricately woven fabric of eighteenth and nineteenth century English usage. Jon feels that with the advance of technology of the twentieth and twenty-first centuries, so much of the textural richness of the language has been discarded and lost. We may well have exceeded the one millionth word in the English lexicon, but, in his words, "a great deal of the colour and clarity of the language of bygone days has been lost in the single minded quest for brevity". He is convinced that the impatient and headlong pursuit of brevity is at least in part the reason why legal documents, for example, seem so incomprehensible to the lay person—a situation that the legal profession may secretly applaud, if not encourage.

Although war stories never seemed to have been of a particular interest to him, the constant bombardment of newscasts dealing with the Gulf War and subsequent military involvements in the Middle East germinated a seed that eventually became *Flight Into Folly.*

He continues writing from his townhouse home in Surrey, Canada and, when time allows, from a wilderness property in the British Columbia Cariboo. He has valiantly attempted to break out of his *minimalist*, short story writing mould by having worked on this: his first novel length story. While this has certainly been a trying departure for him, he has been captivated by the challenge and toils tirelessly on with a new project. Although it seems that writing short stories is still his first love, his attitude appears to be that you *can* teach an old dog new tricks.